WHOM THE GODS WOULD SLAY

By
PAUL W. FAIRMAN

I0616789

ARMCHAIR FICTION
PO Box 4369, Medford, Oregon 97504

*For more information about Armchair Books and products, visit our
website at…*

www.armchairfiction.com

Or email us at…

armchairfiction@yahoo.com

A MARTIAN VIXEN HELD EARTH IN HER SIGHTS

Ordinary women usually give birth to ordinary offspring. But Princess Lall of the planet Mars was far from being ordinary—and her children were even less so. In fact, they were hideous and hungry little things—such was the way of things on Mars. But soon after imposing total devastation upon her home planet, Princess Lall needed a new place to live…and a new place to breed. Her destination? Earth!

But on Earth a mighty Viking, Rolf of the Golden Horn, had been forewarned of Princess Lall's coming. And to stave off her maniacal threat he put together a band of heroes like no other ever assembled. With his brothers-in-arms, one Nubian slave, and the wonder of a new God not yet known to the Viking realms, Rolf and his cadre set out on a journey to the unknown with only one magic wolf's paw and a grand notion of saving the world.

FOR A COMPLETE SECOND NOVEL, TURN TO PAGE 113

CAST OF CHARACTERS

ROLF OF THE GOLDEN HORN
Chosen to save Earth from an alien atrocity, this paragon of Viking strength was definitely in it to win it.

HANGRA THE WITCH
Banished long ago to live alone in the uplands of her country, this notorious witch had seen the future…and trembled.

PRINCESS LALL
A mishap of Martian evolution, she was aggressive and wanton, wanting only the best for her "children"—the masses be damned!

LARS
The subtle change in his stalwart leader was unsettling. He feared that it was only the first of many yet to come…

ROLLO
As fierce a Viking as ever was. How was it that a dark-eyed southern girl and her crucified God turned his head from home?

TAZOR
Being a Nubian slave had taught him much. His quiet contemplation and insight proved vital to the Viking's mission.

LORK
He watched, and when he saw the end to Mars as inevitable, he sent a warning to Earth—but who, if anyone, would receive it?

BOOK ONE
Rolf of the Golden Horn

KNUTE SWENGORSEN had walked many miles inward from the *norsevillage* by the *fjord.* It had been a long, hard climb up the rocked and timbered mountainside. But Knute had moved swiftly, eager to scan the obscene face of Hangra, the witch who had long since been driven into the uplands by the decent folk who lived beside the sea.

Now, weariness was upon him, and he climbed with a curse for each sharp rock, and a more potent curse for the hag who made herself so inaccessible to a man seeking the boon of her dark powers. Thus, a black mood rested upon him as he clambered up the last thorny slope and stood before the squat, teetering hovel of the far-famed witch.

There was no one there to greet him. He scowled and his voice rang across the lonesome crags: "Ho, foul mother! Show yourself before I smash to bits this rotten sty you live in!"

His answer was a somber cackle from off to the left. He whirled and looked among the rocks until he saw her, crouching atop a great boulder. It seemed a stupid place for even a witch to rest, and Knute called out, "Come down, you hag! Did one of your phantom beasts drive you aloft?"

Hangra had eyes of breathtaking beauty. But these eyes were surrounded by a ghastly ruin of scrawny, wrinkled flesh. She was little more than a sack of sparse bones draped over with a shapeless, evil smelling gown. Hair, greasy and matted, obstructed her vision as she peered down at the blond Northman.

"I was studying the stars," she said.

The inanity of this cheered Knute Swengorsen. "Old fool! It is high noon and there are no stars. Have your brains finally rotted beyond all use?"

There was no hostility in Hangra's reply. "The stars do not vanish in sunlight from those whose eyes are sharp. One steeped in the lore may read them night or day."

Knute threw back his head and roared with laughter. "And what say the stars, old crone?"

"They speak of evil—of dark and dreadful things; of a voyage across the void from star to star; of an evil ten thousand years in the making; a devil's nightmare now about to bloom."

"You talk in silly riddles. Voyages from star to star. If such rot were really true, it could still bring no harm to us."

Only now did Hangra flare in anger. "The earth also is a star, you thick-skulled ass! This horror I see concerns us very much."

"Call me not an ass, foul mother," Knute growled, "or I'll pluck you from that rock and twist your throat. Get down here now and serve me. I came to get a potion."

HANGRA'S EYES remained upon the blue heavens and her thoughts were far away. Then she closed her eyes and sat as one possessed by a vision. "As strange a ship as I have ever seen," she whispered. "A ship not built to sail on sea or land. Fire pours from its bowels, and it rides a flaming tail across the skies."

She ceased speaking. Her ancient frame trembled from the tension of her trance. She moaned; then spoke again in a curious singsong voice that chilled the Norseman standing down below.

"I cannot see the substance. It wavers, thick as mist, before my eyes. But all the evil essence I can sense. It rides within that ship. It comes this way across the void." Hangra trembled even more violently and clenched her bony hands as if in anguish. "But I cannot tell if it be man or god!"

There was a time of utter silence. Gripped with a feeling akin to terror, Knute stood dumbly watching the trembling hag. The breeze had ceased to blow. The trees hung motionless. Not a birdling twittered in the air.

Then again, the croaking of Hangra's tortured voice: "Not man. No man has ever learned to ride the void. And if not man—then a god." She stood suddenly erect and pushed her scarecrow arms above her head. "A god! To loose a horror on the earth. All men will die!"

A shriek, as of great pain, was ripped from Hangra's dried and twisted lips. Then she fell to the surface of the great boulder and lay as though dead.

Knute Swengorsen glanced uneasily about him and drew a short-sword half from the scabbard at his belt. He knew a fear, and sought to allay it by striking at some foe. But there was no foe; no one at which to strike. He looked again at the still, black form on the boulder. "Wake up, witch Hangra," he growled. "Awake and brew my potion. I'd be away from here."

And Hangra did awaken upon the sound of his voice. She sat up, looked around her as if in wonder, then came down from the boulder with such ease of motion and so swiftly, that she did not appear to move. She stood before Knute, leaning heavily upon her cane. Her face was drawn and white.

But with the passing of a moment, she was herself again. And around Knute Swengorsen, the forest whispered, the breeze played with the grasses, and the birds resumed their chirping. Knute shook his head as though to clear away the vapors of a brain-mist. He towered threateningly over the withered crone.

"I thought I saw you standing on yon boulder. I'd have sworn I heard you mouthing weird insanities. Yet you stand here. Was that some spell you cast, old witch?"

SHE WALKED around him, utterly without fear, stood in the doorway of her hut and regarded him through eyes of great beauty; eyes like green jewels moulded into an obscene setting by some devil's craftsman. She leered at his bewilderment and said, "What would you have, Knute Swengorsen?"

"Are you deaf? Four times I told my want. A potion such as only you can make."

"Then are many potions—for many purposes."

Knute Swengorsen dropped his eyes like a sullen child. "Mine must be strong and swift. One day now—maybe tomorrow—Rolf comes again to the *fjord*. Even now his galley may be sighted."

"Rolf of the Golden Horn?"

"What other Rolf could I be speaking of?"

"I heard he died in some far land to the south."

"Not true. I'd heard that also. But word came overland."

"How could word come overland from such a far place?"

"It was brought by a band of strange men. They wore gowns, like women, but of coarse and heavy stuff. Fools in women's clothing who tried to make us kneel on the ground and pray."

"I've never seen such men."

Knute sneered at her. "They would have no intercourse with witches. They carried crosses on their staves and told us of a God who died upon a cross."

"What God was this?"

Knute Swengorsen waved an impatient hand. "It doesn't matter. We killed the men before they could tell us much. The news about Rolf they told before."

"What news?"

"Rolf left with Rollo, full a year ago. They went to slay and pillage in the southern lands."

"That I knew."

"According to these women-men, both Rolf and Rollo traveled far into a land called Gaul, I think they said. They burned and killed."

The old hag grinned. "And filled their galleys up with priceless loot I'll wager."

"But Rollo drank of alien wines that turned his blood to water. They traveled until they came to a city walled in stone. There Rollo took a dark-eyed wife and swore he'd never ride the sea again."

"Rollo? Not to return?"

"Not to return. But Rolf refused the bait. He spat upon Rollo and turned the prow of his galley north." Knute waxed even more sullen. He sank to the ground and sat poking the earth between his thick legs. "So now I want a potion, witch."

HANGRA threw back her head and cackled. "I think I see the plot. With Rolf's returning, your chance of fair Freya's hand grows remote indeed. You know full well she'll never bed with you."

"Silence hag! One word more and I'll slice your skinny neck."

Hangra ignored this. "Does the Golden Horn also await Rolf's return ?"

"It hangs upon the wall," Knute growled. "Within the Common House."

"And none but Rolf has ever drunk it dry?"

"None."

"What potion would you have me brew?" she asked.

"A simple one for your foul alchemies. Something to put into the Golden Horn so that when Rolf drinks, it will knock him to the earth. One draught of ale and he falls—"

"And dies?"

"Not death, you fool. It's ridicule I want. Something to destroy the myth of his manhood. With the *norsevolk* laughing at him, I'll take my chance that Freya's love will cool."

Hangra's eyes flashed with scorn. "The day you get sweet Freya into bed, my wolves will mate with doves!"

Knute sprang to his feet and raised a fist over Hangra's head. But the witch stood her ground and laughed with fresh contempt. "I'll not make your potion," she said, and turned away.

But then she stiffened and turned slowly backward, facing Knute. But she did not appear to see him. Rather, her eyes stared through his great bulk and seemed to be reading something written on the hills beyond. She held up a bony finger and spoke—but not to Knute Swengorsen. Rather to the trees and hills and the high blue sky above.

"A potion in the Golden Horn. Why not?"

Knute grinned. "I knew your senses would appreciate the joke."

"You'll swear it is for his lips and his alone?"

"Fool crone! What man would dare use Rolf's great drinking horn?"

"True words." But Hangra still was deep in thought.

"Well, witch. Do I get my potion? I have gold to pay."

"I'll brew the draught."

"And it will do the deed?"

Hangra cackled and rubbed her hideous hands together. "Beyond your boldest dreams. Now sit you down and rest while I prepare the pot."

Knute Swengorsen lowered himself to the surface of a rock and watched Hangra disappear through the dark doorway of her hovel. He lounged in comfort, foreseeing in his mind the sweetness that would be his with Rolf thoroughly discredited. Certain he was that Hangra's potion in Rolf's ale would do the trick. How could Freya do otherwise than foreswear a man turned into a laughing stock? He'd have her in his arms before the new moon rose.

His attention was caught by the sound of movement within Hangra's hut. Then came an odor, stinking, as from a musty cellar of rotten frogs. And Hangra's voice like bone scraped on bone as she chanted some dread spell.

BUT THERE was more to come. Night fell with the seeming swiftness of a blanket drawn across the sky and Knute stared in terror—helpless to move—as a ghastly, blood red glow emanated from the doorway of the hovel. And Knute Swengorsen knew the witch was not alone. There was the sound of muted voices—then a moan of devils, snarling as though loathe to obey some command of the powerful witch within. The red glow dimmed and brightened, to throw a huge shadow of Hangra's twisted form as she moved back and forth about her strange business.

Then it was done with. The blood glow faded and the crone came forth bearing a small vial. "Put this into the drinking horn," she said. "The quantity is minute. But the eighth part of a tiny drop. It will not be seen."

His courage returning, Knute snatched the vial from her thin fingers and thrust it into his belt. Also from his belt, he took forth a bag that jingled pleasantly and held it out.

"Your money, witch. Take it. I would hasten home. This crawling place plays tricks upon my eyes."

Hangra stepped backward. "Begone. And take your gold with you. Evil though you are, you've done the world a service coming here. Back to your village, and take care lest the wolves feed on your flesh."

Knute laughed. "I have no fear of mountain wolves, old crone."

Hangra watched him stride down the rocky slope. Then she looked upward, into the dark sky, and muttered, "No fear of mountain wolves. But what of those that hover in the void?"

After Knute Swengorsen faded from sight, Hangra went back to the high boulder where she sat for a long time watching a great red star low on the horizon.

Soon a chill wind came up and moaned through the trees. With it, the cold moon. Then a shadow flitted softly over the boulder and a white-fanged wolf was there to crouch at Hangra's feet. Without thought, her hand went out to stroke its head.

The wolf licked the hand, straightened and stood staring in the direction Knute had gone. The gray beast whined and wagged its haunches. The wagging was a plea.

But Hangra slapped the wolf across the nose, and spoke sharply: "Curb your appetite, my friend. That, or hunt elsewhere in the woods this night. He is not to be touched. You hear my words? Not to be touched."

The wolf snarled and slunk away. Hangra called after it: "His meat is far too precious for your gullet. He carries the fate of the world within his belt."

She turned to continue gazing, in dreadful fascination, at the low red star.

ROLF OF the Golden Horn was heading home. The winds and the forty oars were driving the prow of his loot-laden galley ever northward; out of the wide mouth of the Gaelic river; swift past the isles of Engle-Land; hard into the waters of the cold Northern Sea and up under the shadows of the great lights that flamed down from the top of the world.

Rolf was going home.

In his heart was a strange mixture of sorrow and happy anticipation. Sorrow at the weakness of Rollo, beside whom he had sailed—to sack, burn, and pillage, even to the gates of Alexandria in the warm southern seas. Together—their galleys breasting the waves side by side—they had prowled far down to the warm and perfumed lands, to sink their swords deep into the rotting corpse of decadent Rome. Side by side, they had gloried in being Vikings! Laughed deep in their throats at the prayer that went up all over Europe to the Man of Galilee and his Father which was in heaven: "From the fury of the Vikings, O Lord, protect us."

Laughed at the gentle prophets; pillaged and burned as they put their faith in the thunder gods and the great-breasted lightning goddesses of the northlands. Spat their contempt on all things weak.

Then, for Rolf, the shock.

Rollo—one day in Gaul, as they cut their way through the defenders of a gray-stone town—raising his sword above a kneeling figure; lifting his great blade high to slash in twain the frail body of a youth.

Then Rollo saw. Not a youth. A dark eyed girl, with breasts scarcely swelling the surface of the white tunic she wore. She knelt before him and in her hands was a small gold cross. Her body was erect from knee to head—straight as a northern pine she knelt. Her face was calm and there was no fear in her eyes.

Still marveling now, Rolf remembered what he saw. Rollo's blade pulled short in mid-air. Then lowered to his side. Rollo's hand reaching down to lift the maid up by her rich, dark hair.

Rollo's voice: "Do you think that bit of gold will save you, maid?"

"I think it will," she answered, steadily. "But kill me if you will—it matters not. Strike. With my final breath I'll pray for you."

AND ROLLO—with a weariness to his voice Rolf had never before detected: "Be silent, maid. I'm not in need of prayers—" But the words and the tone did not match as Rollo released his grip on the girl's hair and touched her gold cross with his fingertip. "There is no strength in this bauble."

"The strength of Him who died upon a cross."

Rollo had turned to Rolf, sheathing his sword the while. "I tire of this. I'll go and rest myself." Then to the girl: "Come, maid, and tell me of this fool you worship. This God who allowed himself to be crucified."

Rollo had been strange from that day on. Keeping to himself and showing no interest in the sharing of the loot. One day, he came to Rolf's tent walking side by side with the girl, her hand in his. "My weariness still persists. I'm tired unto death of pillage, fire, and screams of agony. Even now I fear the worst—that blood will flow in rivers through my dreams."

"Then we'll go home," Rolf told his sailing mate. "I too am lonesome for the high, white peaks. We'll turn our galleys north."

"You must return without me. I'll take me here a wife and here I'll stay. Farewell to you, Rolf. And may your own wild gods have pity and blot your crimes from out your memory."

"My gods are your gods, too."

"Not so. Mine died in Galilee." And Rolf saw the cross suspended around Rollo's neck.

Rollo extended his hand, but Rolf turned away in bitterness. Next day he sailed.

And now, facing again the peaks of his homeland, his heart was troubled with uncertainty as he marveled at the power of the dark-eyed maid who'd bent the fierce Rollo in her hands like a slender twig.

But uppermost were his thoughts of Freya, the golden-haired Norse-maiden he'd left standing on the shore a full year back. Filled as he was with contempt for the slender dark-eyed women of the south, Freya's image gleamed in his memory, quickening his heart and the breath within his throat. Rollo could turn into a milk-white thing if he chose; could take a spindling maiden as his bride.

Rolf smiled. A woman awaited him! A tall and golden maiden built for ecstasy. Broad of bosom, strong of limb. Born and bred to withstand the first, full, glorious shock of mating.

His kind of woman!

Rolf's thoughts were broken now by a shout from the bow of the galley. The thundering voice of Lars, his second in command and his good friend: "Rolf—out ahead! We've raised the points beyond the *fjord*. We're home!"

ROLF HURRIED up the runway upon each side of which twenty slaves bent their broad backs to the oars. They were a mixture, these slaves. Picked for their girth and sinew from a dozen conquered ports, their skins, were black and yellow and white. Some wore great shocks of hair. Some, but a thin black pigtail down their backs. And others bald as gourds. Each was as strong as several ordinary men but none could break the chains that held each to his place. Their backs were broad. But still they feared the whip that lashed them on.

Rolf passed the slaves and went into the prow of the dragon-galley to stand beside Lars and peer across the green waters. "By Tor, you're right! I see the *norsevolk* gathered there!"

And this was true. The galley had been long since sighted. The *norsevolk* lined the shore. Lars, his great red face aglow, waved an arm, then laid it over Rolf's shoulders and said, "I envy you, my friend—for the prize that waits you there."

Rolf's smile was small and tight as, suddenly, a bleak, depressing mood came over him. "She's probably forgotten me," he muttered. "Wed now, no doubt, and waiting with an infant in her arms."

Lars' laughter rang against the hills and back. "Not Freya! That lass will bed with you or die a virgin. How many have tried to turn her heart away from you and failed?"

The *fjord* was now abeam. Rolf said, "You'd best take the rudder, Lars. Bring her on the beach and then set the slaves to unloading."

This disappointed Lars. "I'll run her in, but let the others take care of the rest. I vow I'll see you drain the Golden Horn."

Rolf's smile deepened. "So be it. You and I shall seek the Common House."

The galley was beached skillfully, while the whole *norsevillage* gave shouts of welcome. Rolf's Viking crew tumbled ashore, many to seize yellow-haired wives—to sweep them up and carry them back to the village, each with a line of children strung out behind like a joyful tail. Lovers clung in passionate embrace, and there was not a Viking who did not find a pair of waiting arms.

None except Rolf.

FOR FREYA did not shout welcome with the rest. She stood apart, and as Rolf approached her she smiled but made no move. Nor did Rolf consummate his year-old dreams by seizing her. A peculiar silence gripped him, a shyness he had never known before. He merely held his cupped hands forth and said, "I brought you these."

Her eyes were for him and not the savagely gotten loot. "They matter not," she said softly. "You brought yourself unwounded and alive; that is enough."

But the hands of Freya's mother, gnarled and worn, reached out. Her old voice remonstrated with her daughter: "Be not so ungrateful! Jewels, rings and pendants from far lands. The ransom of a king and you spurn it. Are you mad?"

Rolf's eyes were still on Freya's face. They remained there as he opened his hands and spilled the baubles into those of the *Norsemother*. Some missed the open palms and the old woman was on her knees scrabbling feverishly in the dirt.

But Rolf and Freya saw none of this. Rolf said, "You waited?"

"Had you ever cause to doubt?"

He dropped his eyes like a bashful stripling. "I was so far away. You are warm and young and beautiful. Your loins must have cried out for mating. And you had no way of knowing I'd return."

"I'd mate with no one else. That you should know."

Rolf was now afire to take her to himself and have her. The passion choked in his throat and strangled his words. "Then even today? This night?"

Freya's eyes clouded. "So you may take the sea again at dawn?"

Rolf moved closer and she held her ground until her breasts were hard against his plate. And in his dizziness Rolf heard a voice. The voice was his, but not the words. The words were those of Rollo, spoken back in Gaul, but they came from Rolf's lips as though entirely undirected by his brain.

"I tire of war. I'm through with pillage, fire and screams of death. Even now I fear the worst—that blood will flow in rivers through my dreams."

Her eyes lighted and now her lips came close. "Fear not about your dreams, my love. From this day on I'll take full charge of them. Your time of steel is through. My heart will be your buffer in the night."

"This night?"

"We'll say the vows and spread the marriage feast. Tonight I will be yours."

Rolf let out a mighty shout. "Lars! Jorgen! Nels! Give gifts to all! Gems, gold and silks! And pass the word to lay the wedding feast!"

LARS, EACH arm filled with a yellow-haired maiden, gave also a lusty roar. Arising from where he sat, he dumped both maidens to the ground and said, "By Tor! I've waited a long time for this! Unload the ship. Give wealth and loot to all! Rolf of the Golden Horn will soon be wed."

Immediately, the Viking crew approached from all sides. They laid hands on Rolf and carried him away to his dwelling place. As was the custom, the maidens did likewise with Freya; vanishing with her into the village, to the accompaniment of much laughter.

At Rolf's dwelling place, the Vikings crowded around and horns were raised, filled full with foaming ale. A horn was pushed toward Rolf and it was Knute Swengorsen who remembered.

"Hold there, fool! Is all custom to be forgotten? Rolf should go first to the Common House. The Golden Horn stands waiting to be drained."

This indeed was the custom. A chieftain's worth was measured greatly by his ability to consume the strong ale of the *norsevolk*. And in all the *norseland,* there was no horn so huge and heavy as that of Rolf's. Twice Rolf had stood at the board in the Common House, held the Golden Horn aloft, and emptied it with a single, superhuman draught. This while other Vikings stood by in silent envy. For this feat, more than for any other, they granted him his role as leader. But he could not rest on laurels won before. Fresh off the sea, custom demanded that he repeat the act and thus prove anew his strength.

Rolf eyed Knute Swengorsen and his smiling ceased. He had no liking for this man. A coward, Knute, as evidenced by his land-locked feet. Never had he ridden a galley south in search of loot and glory. He preferred to remain behind and plead suit to lonesome maidens. Weak and cowardly, he had the friendship of no man. To frustrate Knute Swengorsen more than for any other reason Rolf said, "I'll drink at the wedding feast—and not before."

This did not suit Knute Swengorsen. "Could it be you doubt your strength? It would seem you wish to get the maid Freya safely bound to you before you risk your prestige."

Rolf scowled and stepped forward. Drawing his sword, he slapped it flat across his tormentor's rump. "But for the fact that I refuse to kill upon my wedding day, I'd spill your rotten blood. Away, landcrab! And leave this place to men."

Lars dropped his horn and snatched out his own blade. "I'm not being wed today," he cried, "so I claim the joy of slaughtering this cow. I'll tie my hands and lie upon my back and fight him with a sword between my toes."

Rolf, his good spirits revived, stepped forward, laughing. "We'll have no blood to mar this wedding stag."

"I'll tie my legs and fight him with my teeth. He can use two swords."

Rolf roared, "Enough. I claim a drink from all."

THE VIKINGS raised their horns. Lars scowled, then grinned and sheathed his sword as Knute Swengorsen went quickly out the door. A horn was pushed toward Rolf. He drained it and a cheer went up.

Then Lars called, "Silence! I have a tale. A story you'll all like—of love in Gaul. The night we razed their shores, I found two maidens on the rocks—sisters, I vow, who were bathing in the surf. Such terror in four eyes I never saw. Such abject haste to grant my every wish."

A dozen Vikings laughed and one man said, "The details, Lars. You left a sadder pair?"

"Sadder? But no! I'll tell you more of it…"

He settled to his tale. The stag was on.

The hours passed swiftly until, at sunset, Rolf told his vows to Freya by the tree where all the *norsevolk* marriages were made; told them, not knowing of the bitter days ahead. Freya vowed also. Then a maiden bent to shred up Freya's gown—to tear it fore and aft from hem to waist. This symbolized the giving of the bride and they were wed.

Next was the Common House; laughter and ale and food under the yellow light from the great fish oil lamps. Shouting, the Vikings—men who sailed the seas, as differentiated from the *norsevolk* who stayed at home—seated Rolf and Freya on a throne at the end of the groaning table. Shouting, they brought forth the Golden Horn and filled it to the brim with ale. This horn was twice the size of all the rest. Encrusted with jewels and brimming with the brew, it made a weight to break a camel's back.

They handed it to Rolf. The Viking Chief stood tall and lifted the horn on high. All eyes were on him now, and silence settled over the Common House. Twice prior, they had seen him do this thing. But still the thought was in their minds: No man can empty it!

Lars, as though sensing the trend of their minds, got to his feet and cried, "No man but Rolf!"

Rolf took a breath that added a full five inches to the girth of his barrel chest. He put the horn against his lips and drank. The level of the ale went down the horn and, as it sank, each Viking came slowly from his seat as though drawn erect by the falling of the brew. Down—down it went, and higher, even higher, was the tilt of the great cup in Rolf's hands.

Then, with victory seeming sure, Rolf faltered. He swayed. His blue eyes glazed. His grip faltered on the horn. The vessel tilted backward, crashed down with a ringing sound and rolled across the floor.

ALL THE Vikings stood frozen in surprise—all save Lars. His chair fell over as he rushed to Rolf's side past Freya's reaching arms. But Rolf stiffened and scowled and motioned Lars away. But only to reel and grope; to fall forward like a windblown tree and lie as though dead.

Freya knelt down beside him. The Vikings crowded forward. And, shouldered out by the sea-roving giants, the *norsevolk* clustered in the background and spoke among themselves.

They had doubted his ability to empty out the horn. And yet their surprise and consternation was just as great that he had failed. One by one, two by two, and in groups, they went silently out of the Common House as though they felt themselves the humiliation Rolf would know when he awakened.

Now only Freya, Lars, and a dozen Vikings remained. To the Vikings, Freya raised accusing eyes. She said, "You yourselves betrayed him! You let him drink too much at your stupid stag! How could he dry the Golden Horn with forty horns of ale already drunk?" She cradled Rolf's great head in her lap and wept.

One of the Vikings answered her: "He drank but little at the stag. The warmth of southern climates must have softened him."

Lars raised his head and snorted like a bull. "The man who said that better be prepared to fight!" he roared.

The incautious Viking dropped his eyes in confusion as Lars' hand went toward his blade. But Freya frowned. "Have done with words. All this bravado gets us nothing. Help me lift him to his bed."

As the Vikings lifted Rolf and carried him to his dwelling, Lars walked behind with Freya, muttering the while. "There's something rotten here. Rolf could swill ale 'til dawn and walk away. He could laugh with every Viking stiff beneath the board. But to keel over like a stripling in the sun! This smacks of Hangra's work!"

"But she was driven upland long ago," Freya protested.

"Still—many know the pathway to her door."

The Vikings laid Rolf upon his bridal bed. Then, lowering their eyes, they went away. Freya sat long and silently beside her snoring husband. Lars left, to return at a later hour. His face was grim and he was wiping dark blood from his sword.

"He still sleeps?"

"Far deeper than before. It seems that he has just begun to sleep."

"And so does Knute Swengorsen. But for a far longer time, unless he has a means of rising from the dead."

"What made you seek Knute Swengorsen out?"

"Because he was the only enemy Rolf had in the village. Knute yearned to wed with you himself. That I've known for a long time. At the point of my blade he told a tale to make a man sick. He got a potion from the witch Hangra and put it in the Golden Horn."

"You killed him. Now death has marred my wedding night."

"Say rather just execution of a cow not fit to live. You'd best lie down beside your husband and share his dream this night, so long as there is nothing else to share. I have a trip to make into the mountains."

"You waste your time. Hangra cannot be slain by mortal man. Her savage wolves would tear your vitals out."

Lars scowled. "Rest with your husband, maiden, and leave the work of men to men. I yearn to stain my sword with the blood of a witch."

BOILING with rage, Lars left the *norsevillage* and moved toward the uplands further from the sea. The way was sharp and hard, but a pale moon lit the hills and Lars' expanding anger drove him on.

Halfway to Hangra's hut, a shadow fell across Lars' path. The shadow materialized into a wolf, snarled, and slashed with razor fangs at Lars' thigh.

The Viking's sword cut a silver path through the moonlight; a low-swung arc, and the wolf screamed like a soul dipped in hell's hottest brimstone. It slavered in fear and skulked away on three legs, and upon the path in front of Lars lay a severed wolf's foot.

Lars bent and picked it up. The blood, fast running from the ankle, dripped to the ground and then all the blood was gone. But, strangely, under the soft fur gripped in Lars' hand, there was a strong, even pulse beat as though the thing still lived. Lars thrust the paw into his belt and strode on up the mountain.

More shadows came—to turn into gray bodies, hate-filled eyes, great mouth-caverns, filled with fangs. Lars' sword slashed out again and again, but the wolves were careful now. They slipped like water away from his blade, but ever to whirl and come at him again.

Finally, in a great spasm of frustrated rage, Lars dropped his sword and seized the closest beast in his doubled fists. The creature had leaped at his throat and he caught it full in the air, its jaws agape. His hands wrapped true around the jaws, both top and bottom. Then, his legs set wide apart, he tore the beast asunder with one great retching of his muscled chest, until it hung lifeless, split from snout to belly.

"Take that and dine on it, you fiends," Lars yelled, and hurled the carcass at the circling wolves. They fell upon it like the wolves they were, and Lars climbed on. But, strangely, in his belt, the wolf paw continued with its steady, even beat.

Lars found Hangra on the boulder where she seemed to spend much time these days. He drew his sword and hailed her in a ringing voice. "I'm going to kill you, witch! The potion for the Golden Horn was no doubt Knute's idea. But you must share the guilt with him and die. Even now great Rolf lies in a stupor from your handiwork."

SHE watched him from the rock above, her green eyes smouldering with an abstract fire. "The potion Knute desired and the one he got were entirely different," she replied. "Nor should you blame poor Knute Swengorsen too much. He was but what he was, a weak mortal shell. And his visit to my hut was in reality long foreordained."

"You speak in silly riddles. You try to fend off my wrath with words. Come down and meet your fate."

Hangra came to her feet and her green eyes burned. "Silly Viking!"

"I tore your wolves asunder with my bare hands. I sent them slinking into the brush. And now I'll slay their evil mistress."

Her smile was a twisted leer as she replied. "You had no cause to kill my pets. They were a committee of welcome. They sought to lick your face in friendship."

Lars sprang toward the rock, his sword upraised. Hangra croaked, "You cannot slay me, fool! Perhaps you have no fear of my poor powers. Would this reshape your views?"

She waved her cane. A stream of blue fire welled from its tip to lance out and knock Lars' sword from his grip. This done, the flame formed into a hissing, crackling spiral that wrapped around him, forming a cage.

"Stand where you are, Viking! Move not an inch. To touch that fire with so much as a fingertip will spell your death."

Lars stared in wonder at the quivering flame, then heard Hangra's words continuing: "I have no wish to see you stiff in death. And as to Rolf, have you no fear. He sleeps in order that he may fulfill a destiny in which you'll share. Rolf has become a chosen one of forces far beyond your ken or mine. He will awaken soon, so return to your village, for you carry with you a talisman you both will need. A magic tool to guide you on the way you both must go."

Lars' rage had faded and great wonder took its place. He pulled, frowning, at his beard. "There's something here too deep for me." He studied Hangra, then hastened to add: "Think not for a moment that I fear this blue-fire cage. Were I still so inclined, I'd walk right through it and cut your heart from its place in your skinny chest."

Hangra grinned ever so slightly. "That I know full well, brave Viking, and I consider myself fortunate that I have talked you out of such a deed."

Lars pondered. "Yes, your words, while I don't understand them, seem ponderous and full of wisdom. You promise that no harm will come to Rolf?"

"I promise nothing of the sort. It is not within my power. Both he and you may die. We all may die. Return to your village now. You'll find he's learned much that you should know."

As though having forgotten the fire, Lars stooped to pick up his sword. Hangra's hand moved slightly, and the fire bent away from him in all directions; then it faded into nothingness.

Lars, deep in thought, sheathed his weapon and turned down the hill. He walked slowly and came to a halt as Hangra's voice pursued him: "Guard well the wolf paw in your belt. You'll find that Rolf knows what to do with it."

Lars continued on and anyone within earshot could have heard him muttering, "It's not that I was afraid. It's just that discretion is a part of valor that should not be overlooked. When one fights demons, one only does the best one can. One strives to stay alive."

He increased the speed of his lagging feet now, and was suddenly conscious of the wolf's paw pulsing evenly in his belt.

IT WAS well into the night when he reached the *norsevillage* and went straight to Rolf's dwelling place. All was quiet as he pushed his way into the bedchamber where Rolf lay. As before, Freya sat by the bedside, waiting patiently for her husband to awaken. Rolf's huge form lay quiet on the bed.

But, as though Lars' entrance was a signal, Rolf stirred, and Freya leaned quickly forward. "His eyes are opening," she whispered. "He is awakening."

This was true. As Lars and Freya watched, Rolf sat up and looked around the chamber. There were signs of great bewilderment in his expression. He passed a hand across his forehead and asked, "How came I back so quickly?"

"Back from what place, my love?" Freya inquired of him, "You have not been away. Not since you returned in your galley from the south."

Rolf continued to gaze around him.

"That was long before. Since then I traveled to a strange place—high in mountains so tall they dwarfed the peaks we know here in the Northland."

Freya pressed an anxious question:

"Do you not recall our wedding, Rolf? The feast in the Common House and your drinking from the Golden Horn?"

"Aye, that I remember well, but it was very long ago. Much has happened since."

"It was only yesterday," Lars said.

"Regardless of how things appear to you, the facts are these, and mark them well because they are true. You fell into a faint while drinking from the Golden Horn and we brought you to your bed. For hours, you've lain in a stupor and are just awaking now."

Rolf stared full into Lars' face and the latter stood frozen. It was as if Lars had never seen this man before. Swiftly he scanned the giant Viking's face. The features, taken singly, seemed the same: the jutting hawk's nose; the high forehead; the great mane of golden hair. Yet in assembly, they seemed to mark a different man.

THEN LARS saw what had changed. The eyes. New fires burned within them now. The icy northern blue was gone, and in its place were azure fires reminding Lars of those the witch Hangra had used to trap him in the uplands. And Lars was filled with awe at what he gazed upon and could not understand.

He came forward and placed a hand upon Rolf's knee. "It was a potion in your drink that laid you low—put there by Knute Swengorsen and brewed by Hangra in the hills. Knute Swengorsen I killed, and hastened up the mountains to do the same to Hangra."

Lars shifted his eyes and split his telling so that Freya was also included. "But I came upon strange things. There is more to this than Knute Swengorsen's jealousy. Hangra spoke of things foreordained, and in the telling, I got the feeling she is not so evil as we've always thought. Now tell us what occurred within your dream."

Rolf got up and stretched his mighty legs. "I must go forth and slave an evil god," he said.

Tears came to Freya's eyes. "Somehow I knew, there in the Common House, that wedded ecstasy was not for me. What god is this that you must slay, and why?"

"Come," said Rolf.

He led them from the dwelling place and stood in the open gazing at the sky. For a time he stared only at the moon; then gave this over and let his eyes wander across the star-filled heavens, stopping now and again to study some intricate pattern upon the inverted surface of the dark-blue bowl above. Then he raised his arm and pointed to a large red star close to the horizon.

"The god comes from there," he said. "I traveled far with Hangra in my dream. Just how it was done, I do not know, but I learned many things. She showed me somewhat of how things are made; knowledge I did not have before. She showed me that the stars are not just pinpricks in the night where light comes through, but worlds like ours upon which people live."

Both Lars and Freya were silent. All this was beyond them and smacked of insanity. Yet such was Rolf's intensity, it did not occur to either of them to doubt.

"She showed me then a ship not built for land or sea; a giant tear drop fashioned in a forge and made to sail the void." He was still pointing at the baleful red star. "It came from there," he said, "straight toward our world. And in its hold, there rides this evil god who must be slain. If this god triumphs, earth will end its days, overrun with vermin eating out the life of every living thing."

"What does this god look like?" Lars asked. "And how will all this vermin come to be?"

ROLF FROWNED. "I cannot answer you—I do not know. There was a mist that covered everything. But I saw Hangra's eyes and heard our own gods speak in thunder from the skies. In Hangra's eyes and in the thunder, only this was clear: The evil god must die. I tell you even our gods are afraid and Hangra trembles for the world."

Lars was staring also at the star. "Hangra told me something of this tonight and said I also fitted into the scheme. The details all are news to me, and I will test you now to see if this be truth or just some hoax to fill up Hangra's time."

"What test have you?"

"Tell me—what talisman do I carry that will be needed and how will it be used?"

Rolf did not hesitate: "There is a place flanked with high mountains; the top of the world, it seemed. It is to this place we must go to find the god, and in your belt you have a wolf paw Hangra gave you."

"She gave it not! I took it from her beast."

"She sent her beast. The wolf paw has a pulse beat in it and as we make our way across the sea and land, the paw will show the way."

Freya was weeping quietly. "How?" she asked. "By running on before?"

"No. But if our path be true, the pulse will beat. If not the pulse will fail. We have but to follow—it will lead the way."

"I still don't understand," Freya pursued. "Why was my husband chosen for this mission? And you say our gods are fearful in Valhalla. That cannot be true."

"Our gods are fearful for the world. They are powerless before this alien god."

"And Hangra's magic? That is powerless too?"

"The only power that can destroy this god is a strong right arm and several feet of steel."

Lars had taken the wolf paw from his belt. He handed it to Rolf. "There is your talisman." It lay in Rolf's palm and Freya reached forth and took it. Her eyes widened.

"A paw severed and still beating with the rhythm of a heart. There's much in this to cancel out all doubt. And yet..."

"When do we leave?" Lars asked.

"We've already waited far too long. The time is very short."

"Then I will rouse the men?"

"One man. Call Jorgen only. We must travel fast and light 'cross half a world."

FREYA MOVED close to him, her eyes again brimming with tears. "Is the rush so great that you must leave a virgin bride? Cannot the god-slayer become a husband first and his virgin bride a wife?"

Rolf took her in his arms, then pressed her back. "I will return," he said, "knowing you'll keep yourself for me."

She stood erect and there was misery in her eyes. "That you can always know, for it is truth. But still scant comfort for the one you leave."

But he scarce heard her. He'd turned to Lars and the fever in his own eyes had increased. "The wind is fair and will remain so for a time to come. We raise the sail and ride the waters. That much I know. Bring Jorgen to me in my dwelling place."

Silently, Freya helped her husband dress; wound up the leather thongs that held his leggings on; fastened his belt and then—though it took all her strength—insisted that she lift the great horned helmet; and while he knelt, she put it on his head. Then she had one last word. Simply, she said, "Please do not go, my lord. My heart tells me you will not return; that I will await you, barren, knowing and wanting no other man, 'til I am old and toothless and alone."

Rolf's laughter boomed against the ceiling. "Have no such doubts, sweet wife. I will return when this great deed is done, and we will raise strong sons to sail the seas and bring us wealth in our old age. But go I must."

Freya lowered her head in submission. "Then I will say no more. One kiss, my husband."

They kissed, and as Rolf released his bride, the room seemed full of giants. Lars himself took up a lot of space, but the two with him, added to the bulk of mighty Rolf, seemed to bend the walls of the chamber.

"Here is Jorgen," Lars said. "He understands it not, nor did I bother to explain too much, but he is agreeable."

JORGEN was of the Viking cut. Broad, red-faced, yellow-haired. But in his eyes was a certain bovine look—a dullness as though not too great an intelligence roosted behind them. But none could question the loyalty he gave his Chief.

"My sword is ready," he said. That was all.

But Rolf's attention was held by the fourth man in the room. A giant Nubian who stood with folded arms. Naked to the waist, he appeared to be built of shiny black mahogany. His muscles bulged and rippled beneath his ebony skin.

"This slave I know," Lars said. "I talked with him on the galley coming north. We took him during a raid in Gaul—hauled him off a slave platform where he lay chained."

"But I said bring only Jorgen," Rolf cut in.

"True, but this slave will be valuable. He speaks five languages. He has served many masters in many lands. His tongue would be of use to us."

Rolf considered, then nodded his head. "You are right, but no man goes on this journey as a slave." Turning to the Nubian, Rolf said, "What is your name, fellow?"

"Tazor is what I'm called." The Nubian's eyes were flat, expressionless.

"We go on a long and perilous journey, from which all of us may not return. Do you wish to go with us, sharing our hardships and our rewards—as a free man?"

"I was taken as a slave at four," Tazor replied. "My father was a slave and his, and his again. Freedom I never had so I do not know whether I'd have use for it or not. But I will go with you and do my best."

"Strike off his chains," Rolf said. "Give him a belt and weapons and a cloak."

The Nubian was supplied. Water and ale and food were put upon the ship. Rolf kissed his wife again as Tazor raised the sail. Then, with a mighty push, Rolf sent the galley off the sand—into the sea—to follow it and climb aboard.

The freshened pre-dawn winds filled the dragon-canvas and the galley sheared to the south as Jorgen laid the rudder over hard. White water chopped across the prow.

Then, in the faint false dawn, the sharp eyes of the Viking Rolf beheld a figure on the rocky point beside the *fjord;* saw Freya's hair streaming in the breeze, her arm upraised. Heard her call out, "Farewell, god-slayer. May fortune favor you!"

"I will return," Rolf called. Then he turned his eyes forward and never again looked back.

DAY AFTER day came up at dawn to pass and sink into the western sea. Rolf paced the walk between the empty galley benches and grudged each passing hour. Lars, too, seemed impatient.

"The land crawls by," Rolf growled. "Would that we had a ship the like of which I saw within my dreams."

Lars shrugged. "Wishing is of no help. We can but bide our time and hope our talisman proves faithful."

Rolf took the severed wolf paw from his belt. "The pulse beats strong and true."

Lars scowled. "I'll have more faith in that claw when I find it can do otherwise."

The faith of the Viking was bolstered four days later when the land they skirted began to fade away toward the east; when Rolf brought forth the wolf paw and called, "Hold! The beat is fading out. It's almost gone!"

Lars ran forward and found that it was true. "According to this hairy pilot," Lars said, "we've gone off course. What are your orders now?"

"Cleave to land!" Rolf shouted. "Jorgen—over on the rudder! Tazor—bend the sail!"

Upon command, Jorgen brought the rudder hard over, the Nubian hurled his strength against the mast and brought the square sail around until the ship heeled eastward. After a few minutes, Rolf nodded and handed the wolf paw to Lars. Again the beat was strong and even. Lars stared at the grisly trophy in his palm and said, "This thing fair makes my skin creep."

Later, with the stolid Jorgen holding the rudder—as he would hold it, if necessary, until Kingdom Come—the other three were standing in the bow.

"Tell me, Nubian," Rolf said, "do you know anything of these lands we pass?"

Tazor's dark, expressionless eyes played back and forth along the shore. "This, I believe, is the far northern part of the Gaelic lands. We travel to the east, but not the east of spices and of palms. They must be reached much further south as you well know. I have never been this way before, but I think that trouble lies ahead for our ship. I fear the waters end in ice on one side and the vast land from whence came the Mongols on the other."

"The wind holds fair as it has held for days," Rolf said. "According to our talisman, we must go on."

The Nubian looked silently at Lars and Rolf—then said, "You told me when we left the shore that I was free."

"That's true, you are."

"Then I may not be amiss in giving voice to curiosity. I have a natural wonder as to what land you seek—what place we go. Considering the route we take, my wonder increases."

"You have a right to know, my friend. We've kept you in the dark from carelessness, not plan."

IMMEDIATELY, between them, the two Vikings told the Nubian of all that had occurred. The part that Hangra played—the mission she had given Rolf to kill a god in some far place.

Tazor looked flat eyed at the wolf paw, took it in his hand and felt its pulse. His expression did not change. "I long to speak my mind," he said, "but never having been so bold before—"

"Speak out, man," Rolf growled. "What must I do to prove to you you're free?"

Tazor tossed the wolf paw into the air—caught it. "This could be but a trick," he said. "In the bazaars of Alexandria I've seen fakirs turn iron rods to snakes. I've seen a dog beheaded and then go about its business sniffing in the rubble. Yet all was fraud, done by suggestion of the fakir into the minds of those who watched. The witch you tell of could be no more than they. A creature with the ability to creep into men's minds and leave her own will there."

Lars blinked. "The man speaks wisdom. If one grows as wise as this by being a slave, we should all spend a few years in chains."

Tazor's smile was a brief and fleeting thing. "I do not call this fraud. I only say it could be. But as to its being so, there is one point that gives me pause."

"And that?"

"You say this witch told you the earth is round and that all the stars above are also round—other earths we see at night because the sun reflects against them."

"That she told me," Rolf said.

"All that is truth, and no magic is involved. Wise men have discovered these things by human means but are afraid to speak out for fear of being tortured and killed."

"Then Hangra spoke the truth," Lars said.

"That, to me," Tazor said, "is the strange part of it. How this witch in the northern wilds can know these things is far beyond me."

"She is very old," Rolf said. "I have known of her since my childhood. She could have come from some far place."

"Driven away for speaking the truth possibly. But on one point she is in error."

Lars could bend in any direction with the slightest breeze. He said, "Ho! You caught one of her lies? I spotted several myself."

"This god she sent you to slay. He is no god. When the time comes—if it does—for you to drive your sword into him. You will find him flesh. Even though he comes from some far world in a ship we do not understand, he is mortal. That I know."

"And why are you so sure?"

"First, there is the tendency of all mortals to blame all they do not understand on gods. Hangra had wind of something she did not understand and so she calls the perpetrator—this interloper from the void—a god."

"Second, you were selected to oppose him because of your girth and strength. Probably no man on this earth or from any other world could stand before you. But what chance would you with your puny steel—or any of us have—against a supernatural entity?"

Rolf's eyes burned. "Such wisdom from a man who spent his life in slavery!"

"Any wisdom I have gained," Tazor said, with the same quick, fleeting smile, "is probably the result of being forced to keep my mouth shut and listen. One hears much in a lifetime."

ROLF TOOK the wolf paw into his hand and stared at it. "We'll still depend on this," he said.

"Of course. But depend more on what is in your own heart; in the confidence you have in your own destiny. What place was it you saw while in your trance?"

"There were high, rugged mountains, raging storms and flying snow so thick you couldn't see your hand."

"That could be in the mountains north of the Roman boot. Or further east, where the backbone of the world runs like a spine above the land called India."

"But the place we seek," Rolf said, "was bare of snow, and warm. There was broad blue water and a place this ship of space could come to earth."

"India's holy men tell of such places in the highest mountain spine. But how a witch so far away could know—"

Lars yawned, then slapped the Nubian cheerfully upon the back. "Enough of this deep talk. So much wisdom in so short a time fair spins my brain. It's time for food and ale. The rest will keep."

"I am without hunger now," the Nubian said. "I'll take the place of Jorgen. I'm sure he thirsts for ale far more than I."

"My appetite is also gone," Rolf said, and moved toward the bow where he stood deep in thought. Soon he was scowling and in his eyes was a look of bewilderment. He shook his great yellow mane like a bull beset by insects. "Something full strange is happening to me," he muttered.

And truly, it was strange indeed. Since Rolf had awakened from his sleep, his very mind seemed changed. He had become conscious, it appeared, of a new, invisible world within the air. Now and again there were soft, vague whisperings in his ears. And yet not so, but rather in his brain. Not words, spoken in sound, but images of thought, complete and whole, projected from without.

It was as though his mental eyes had been opened to a vast new vista of thought-traffic flowing constantly; but still like whisperings in a dark room. Just now, as the dragon-ship clove west, and Lars went unperturbed about his meal, Rolf felt the impact of a message spanning space. His newfound senses told him it was from the mind of Hangra in the hills. The message came, but it was not for him.

This he knew, because the message was a plea—the calling of a name repeated many times.

Rollo—Rollo—Rollo, far in the land of Gaul. Rollo who has a mighty cross of gold—give ear!

Again and again the image picture came until the bewildered Rolf felt a sense of guilt, as though he crouched to listen by a wall. Suddenly he turned and bawled aloud: "Lars! I have changed my mind. Pour me a horn of ale. I'll drink with you!"

BOOK TWO
The Scourge of Mars

LORK, THE Hermit Scientist of Mars, stood at the highest window of his isolated tower and watched the destruction of a planet. He was a handsome man this Lork, by Martian standards. He stood four feet two inches in height—quite tall. His body was acceptably spindling and insignificant and his magnificent head measured twenty-eight inches from ear to ear. This afforded him a brainpan unmatched in size by any on the planet. Also, the ray examination given by law to all Martians revealed his brain surface as having over a foot of channeling to the square inch. In short, Lork was one of the most notable achievements of a twenty-thousand-year-old civilization. A human brain developed to its ultimate.

His broad face was entirely expressionless as he studied the devastation going on about him—as he looked out over the wide plains stretching in all directions from his tower, to see the solid mass of voracious black destruction.

It came in a great arc, this dark wall, moving ever forward to cover the land with itself. Before it, and disappearing relentlessly under the wall, were the green fields, the forests, the homes, the great farms that had fed all Mars. Here and there on the panorama before Lork, a scattering of Martians in twos, threes, and small groups, staggered across the fields and waded the streams in a vain attempt to avoid their certain fate.

But these last few moved slowly now, their strength almost gone. They were only a handful to the multitudes, almost the entire population of the planet, that had already fallen and been consumed by the black wall during the six awful months of its existence.

Lork, tiring of the distant black monotony, desired a closer look. He shut his eyes and projected a mental reflector across the green area surrounding his tower, thus bringing the moving wall within a few feet of his scrutiny.

The ants, of which it was made up, were jet-black and about five inches in length. They had four legs on each side of their tuberous bodies, and each one possessed a pair of mandibles capable of snapping a fragment of rock into two fragments. Their speed was amazingly swift—a steady forward sweep of slightly over seven miles an hour, and they left nothing in their path. The forward edge of the wall got the cream of the forage, of course, but the hungrier waves coming along behind consumed the very fiber of the trees and the remains of animal structures right down to the last fragment of bone.

The Ants of Lall left behind them only the rock and earth they walked upon.

LORK'S MENTAL processes now were based primarily upon the fact that he could do nothing about this destruction. Therefore, he viewed it with an entirely objective attitude. He was incapable of emotions such as hate, greed, fear, regret, so the approaching moment of his own destruction and that of the few students he housed in his tower, was a matter of no great interest.

No—not entirely true. There was a tinge of regret in his mind, but for the reason that he must die with certain questions unanswered; questions concerning this ant horde of Lall's. Computing swiftly, Lork ascertained to a nicety his own life expectancy. It came to three hours and slightly more than nine minutes. He didn't bother cutting it any finer than that, and immediately turned his mind again to the major question that plagued him.

As a preliminary, he created an immense mental reflector and boarded it, so to speak, for a trip around the planet. The job of destruction, he saw, was almost completed. From pole to pole, the ant hordes lay from three to four inches thick on more than nine-tenths of the planet. The final tenth would soon be covered.

But not quite all of it, and that was what puzzled Lork. As he spanned and respanned the globe, he visited again the tiny sanctuaries, the small havens invariably shunned by the ant hordes. These sanctuaries were of course crowded with Martians. It was amazing to see the ant wall split as one of these small areas was approached, surge around it in two directions, and merge again on the far side. Of course these places were but false security for the refugees crowded into them. The Martians so sheltered would die in the end regardless—die of want and starvation. But the point of interest to Lork was the fact that the ants avoided—without exception—every shrine and place of worship on Mars. These and these alone were the sanctuaries.

This completely baffled Lork's superbly objective and scientific mind. He was not averse to orthodox religion, but neither was he a religious man. He had visited the great shrines and had found the cool interiors restful and refreshing. He had admired the fine works of art on tile altars, but the spiritual significance of these temples of orthodox religion failed to touch him. Even now, with surviving Martians hailing their temporary deliverance as a miracle—knowing beyond all doubt that their god was protecting them—Lork refused to accept this as an answer.

WHY, HE asked himself again and again, do the ants avoid the shrines? He did not wish to die with this knowledge ungained.

He had wrestled with the problem for an hour and a half now, and he was going to have to give it up because there was another question to be answered. This last was not a scientific conundrum, but it interested him nonetheless. It concerned Lall.

Why was she destroying the planet upon which she herself had to live? Was not this the equivalent of suicide? Why was she doing this?

Seeking an answer, Lork projected to that small portion of the planet he had not recently visited; the high polar cap where Lall made her headquarters. She was, of course, in no danger from the ants, nor was her small band of husbands, but she and they depended—as did all other Martians—upon the edible outgrowths of the planet itself. Yet she was destroying the surface of this planet as fast as she could manage it.

Lork was cognizant of Lall's mental makeup. She was enjoying all this immensely. Since the fool Martian Council had banished her to the pole—instead of executing her as Lork had recommended—her great ambition had been to avenge the insult and humiliation. But she was no fool. Certainly she would not do this at the expense of her own destruction. She must have a plan, and Lork yearned, in an entirely abstract manner of course, to know what it was.

He brought his mental projection to bear on the polar cap, arriving there just as Lall, surrounded by her five husbands, approached the vast dome-shaped building around which the other buildings clustered and stood waiting for the door to open.

Lork studied Lall with objective curiosity. He knew what she was, of course; nothing more nor less than a huge queen ant. A most interesting history had preceded her.

She had been born of normal parents—a male and female antedating the great two-hundred-year Improvement Period, that era when the human race was scientifically up-bred just as cattle had been scientifically up-bred generations before, and with just as brilliant results. As cattle were bred for meat, so were humans bred for brain and intelligence. They diminished in stature and broadened in skull capacity and scope of intellect.

There were various phases of experimentation, of course, before the correct formula was hit upon, some of which was to the eternal disgrace of all Mars. This last—in the main— by a clique of scientists who came momentarily into power and attempted to transplant the unerring and little understood instincts of certain insects into the perfect human male and female. They were caught up with and speedily eliminated, these fanatics, and it was believed they did little damage. In fact, their tampering was all but forgotten when—ten generations later—Lall was born to obscure and apparently normal parents.

SHE WAS a throwback of the most startling kind. Physically, she represented the perfect female form of the pre-enlightened age; tall, with smoothly rounded limbs, prominent breasts, and all the facial beauty with which uncontrolled nature endowed females for the purpose of attracting and stimulating males and thus increasing the birthrate. Had this been the entire extent of her peculiarities, she would have been merely a lovely, but rather sad freak. A lonesome beauty in an enlightened age that had no need of female beauty.

But Lall developed other tendencies; sexual appetites that bordered upon the obscene and were thus classed until she was examined by the Martian Medical Board and the truth became known; that the unfortunate creature had borne the brunt of those awful experiments of the long ago. Physically she was a woman, but her offspring assumed a far different shape. Startled doctors were forced clear down the insect gamut to the queen ant in order to find a counterpart to Lall's procreational activities.

Mentally, the insect world had captured her completely. She had the instincts to a nicety—all the cunning and the sadistic cruelty of the ant. These traits, coupled with unusual human intelligence, made her a problem over which the responsible elements of Martian society had to pass judgement.

The verdict was exile, and that verdict, rendered without the authorities knowing of Lall's vast physical resources and procreational powers, set the death seal upon a planet. The execution of that planet was now being carried on.

All this flashed through Lork's mind while he watched Lall as she waited for the door of the great building to open. And also, just before the answer to his second question was revealed.

This answer came when the door opened and he followed Lall and her husbands inside the building; when he saw the ship.

Lork's surprise was deep and genuine because this space ship he was staring at had no legal right to exist. Ten years prior to this time—shortly after the first successful space flight to the smaller of Mars' two moons—space ships and space flights had been outlawed by the Supreme Council as being contrary to the long-range principal of isolationism written into the Second Martian Constitution eleven centuries before.

The four ships known to have existed had been cut up and turned into scrap metal. Or so it had been announced. Evidently, Lall had found a way to corrupt certain public officials.

THIS, HOWEVER, did not interest Lork to any great extent. Of more importance to him was the fact that one of his questions was answered. Lall had no intention of remaining on Mars to starve. She planned, obviously, to leave the dead planet and seek a home somewhere else in the solar system. But where?

This, Lork speedily learned as he moved close to peer over her shoulder while she studied a solar map handed her by one of her husbands. A planet was encircled thereon. The one closest to Mars and slightly nearer the sun. Quite logical, Lork thought.

At that moment, a hand touched Lork's shoulder. He started, glanced around, and was again standing, both physically and mentally, at the high window in his tower. Pralt, one of his students, coughed apologetically as he withdrew his hand.

"Sorry," Lork said, "I was projecting."

"Didn't mean to disturb you. Just wanted to call your attention to the ants. They're almost to the base of the tower. It won't be long now."

Lork glanced down. "You're right. We won't have long to wait. It will be interesting—the experience of death."

"I'm looking forward to it. So are the others."

"By the way, my projection was quite successful. I answered one of the questions."

"Really? Why do the ants avoid the shrines?"

"Not that one. I discovered why Lall is not afraid to destroy Mars. She has a space ship. She is going to the planet called Earth."

"Ah! Official corruption. Too bad there's no use doing anything about it."

"Have you ever been to Earth?" Lork asked.

"No. I've tried, but I've never been able to project that far."

"I made it twice. Very backward planet. Still slicing each other up with knives. Not a bad lot though."

Pralt sighed. "Certainly wish we could figure out why the ants avoid the shrines."

Lork glanced down to where the ants were exploring the lower bastions of the tower. It was only a matter of nine and three-quarter minutes now. "Why don't you work a few more equations on it?" Lork said. "I'd do it, but I'm going to be rather busy."

"Doing what?"

"Trying to warn Earth of Lall's coming. I think I can push some telepathic pictures through."

"But you say they're backward. There won't be a mind on Earth capable of receiving the pictures."

"Maybe not, but it's worth a try. An attempt will satisfy my sense of justice."

"In the meantime, I'll try some advanced theoretical equations on that shrine problem."

THE TWO scientists placidly seated themselves, and each went about his work as the sound of ant mandibles grinding through rock became audible from below. Lork's huge head quivered as he created an electrical field around it. He closed his eyes and his magnificent brain began functioning— creating clear mental pictures and hurling them out into the void. The space ship was excellent material with which to work. It had color and size, two of the pre-requisites for the ideal mental image.

Meanwhile, Pralt sat with folded hands, building and rejecting equations with a speed that turned his thought-channel into a silver blur. Because time was limited, he also adopted a color pattern, designating red as the unvarying clue. That way he could spin the equations through his brain without check and merely watch for a flash of red.

The minutes passed. The sound of a million ant-claws climbing the tower was first a faint whisper; then it became the sound of wind blowing across a field of ripe grain. Now the grinding of ten million jaws as the ants did away with the sashes of the lower windows. The tower trembled. There was a dread and fateful sound in the stair-tunnel outside the door.

Pralt saw a flash of red in his thought train.

Glancing at the door, he flung his mind after the stained equation and dragged it back. If they would only give him a few more seconds. The door shivered, bent like paper, disappeared.

"I've got it," Pralt said. "The shrine is Y shaded—the ant horde, *calandra theorized.*"

Lork rationalized it and allowed himself an instant of mild surprise. "Well I'll be damned," he said. "I'll try and tell Earth."

But he never knew whether or not he succeeded. A moment later he was experiencing the equation of death.

LALL, ALL her evil beauty glowing, fiercely joyful, looked down from the port window of the space ship as it blasted up into the thin atmosphere over Mars. It was a black planet now; a globe covered with crawling, twisting death; a symbol of her triumph—her magnificent revenge.

"Tell the pilot to circle once or twice," she said. "I want to look it all over before we go."

One of the huge-headed husbands who gave her constant attendance, sprang up to relay the order. As the ship leveled away on a fiery tail to skim the black surface below, Lall declaimed for the benefit of her three remaining spouses: "They know now what it means to humiliate me."

The Martian men replied in unison: "Yes, Lall."

"Never was a revenge so complete—so entirely satisfactory."

"No, Lall."

Knowing full well what kept these miserable males in line, Lall turned casually, opened her robe, readjusted and belted it while pretending not to hear the collective catching of their breath.

"That despicable Lork! The one who recommended my death. I would like to have witnessed his final agonies. How he must have writhed and screamed."

"Yes. Lall."

She turned and flung up her lovely arms in a gesture of triumph. "Lork and all of them... That stupid Council. Those doctors who examined me as though I were a freak! The wives who screamed for my death. The husbands who allowed me to be exiled and shamed. All of them died in agony and I rejoice. Do you hear that? Rejoice!"

"Yes, Lall."

She turned again to the window and—looking down—she softened. A tender light came into her eyes. "My ants," she whispered. "My poor, poor ants. Nothing more to eat. No one to watch over them. They too must die."

"Yes, Lall."

"But it will be a worthy death and they will not mind because they love me as I love them." She lowered her eyes under thick, dark lashes and looked like nothing so much as a beautiful virgin, trembling in anticipation of her wedding night. "But there will be more ants. Many more."

The husbands leaned forward and put eagerness into their reply: "Yes, Lall!"

"Now I tire," Lall said. "Tell the pilot I have kissed my brood goodbye. Off to the far planet and new conquests!" Her voice softened. "Tell him also that he will be favored this night."

THE MARTIAN men drooped a trifle upon hearing this, each because of his own personal disappointment. Yet it was perfectly proper, because the pilot was Lall's fifth husband.

"You may leave now," she said. "I would rest."

"Yes, Lall," they replied, and trooped out.

Alone, the ant queen lay down upon her lounge and closed her eyes. She was weary, what with the tremendous strain of arranging everything and the prolonged period of egg laying, which preceded her savage destruction of all living things on Mars.

But even above that, there was *the problem* adding mental strain to the physical. Lall knew without being told—knew from age-old instinct—that continued procreation was as necessary to her as the air she breathed. The law, which governed her existence, was clear on that point: Breed or die. Perpetuate or wither into a husk and blow away.

She found no personal pleasure in this monotonous process and often cried out against her unhappy fate. But nonetheless she was forced to face it and the problems it conjured up.

The greatest of these was males to use in this unending process. She had had a great deal of trouble on that score all during her mature life. Martian civilization had gone through the period of enlightenment long before she had been born, and a great majority of the Martian males looked upon her physical beauty with complete disinterest. The five husbands she now possessed had been gotten only after long and weary searching. And invariably, the Martian male who responded to mere physical beauty was an inferior specimen. This hurt the quality of the eggs she produced, a thing she bitterly resented. Mulling the problem over in her mind, she thought with fierce joy of the ten and twelve inch ants she could produce with virile mating. And also came the gnawing worry relative to the five husbands she had. They would not last much longer. All too soon they would become hollow shells, husks to wither and die as she herself would wither and die if she found no males to replace them.

Then, deeply weary, her eyelids drooped and she slept like a tired, beautiful child.

ROLLO THE Viking was the happiest of men. Not filled with the wild, false happiness he'd come to know in his more violent years, but deeply ingrained now with a contentment he had earned through long hours of penance and meditation.

With sorrow, he had watched his true friend Rolf turn coldly northward; stared with tear-filled eyes as the dragon-ship heeled the breeze and rode away down the wide Gaelic river toward the sea.

But he sent a blessing on the wind to guard the mighty Rolf and see him safely home. Then he turned with a heavy heart toward his own sorry affairs.

So much there was to remember and regret; so many hours of repentant agony to be spent at the foot of the cross before the evil he had done could be atoned. But there were times of great joy, also. These came when he was privileged to pore over the old documents, the priceless parchments that told of Christ the Savior.

To the changed Rollo, each of the carefully scrolled words of the patient monks was a burning symbol; and the meaning of the words and phrases thrilled him to his very soul.

Once his heart had been touched by the magic of the Galilean, he had gone doggedly and methodically about the doing of what had to be done. He had knelt before the good monks and then had arisen to break his sword over his knee. Next, under their direction, his loot had been distributed among the poor until he had not a coin nor a piece of silver.

Then had come the penance; the hours and days on the cold stone before the church clad in but sackcloth with ashes on his head and sorrow in his heart.

Slowly, magically, the cleansing process was completed and came the day the good friar lifted him and said, "Arise, my son and look upon the cross. Your heart is pure."

And such gladness went through the being of Rollo, he could scarce contain it. He looked for one glorious instant upon the glowing symbol of Christianity and murmured, "Oh Lord, I am not worthy," whereupon he again fell to his knees and prayed until the sweat stood out on his great muscles and he was like to faint.

Then he rose up and went about another duty; went straight to the cottage of Madella, the slim girl he'd seen first below his upraised sword and later in a burst of white, revealing light.

He sat beside her and took her hand in his and said, "I came to ask great happiness from you."

She smiled. "My hand?"

He shook his head. "Nay—release from my promise to you."

Her smile faded and there was sadness in her great brown eyes. "You do not love me?"

"It is not that. I think I love you more than any man. But I would take the greatest of all vows. I would vow chastity and service to Him from this day on. I love you well and you love me. But beside our love for Him, all else fades to a feeble glow."

She said, "I understand and I rejoice that I have seen this miracle occur. Such a short time ago, you came from down the river shouting oaths—filled with dark deeds and lusting for our blood. And now I see a saint before my eyes."

He pressed her hand. "Far from a saint. Merely a humble one who wants to serve. Do I have your permission?"

"Go with God. I'll pray for you."

HE KISSED her lips and went back to the church; into the monastery of the monks to stand before the kindly abbey there. "I beg to spend my days within these walls. Give me the meanest duties in your house. I'll mop the floors or plant the land or wash the tired feet of those who work. Command me, Father."

The keen and wise eyes of the abbey studied Rollo's face. His silence lasted while the sun bent down to bathe the room in fire through the deep-stained glass. Then he arose from his chair and told Rollo, "Come with me."

Rollo looked with wonder on the place they went. The abbey smiled and motioned toward the walls. "There," he said, "is our greatest treasure; the books and scrolls and manuscripts on which our faith is based. The word of God told in many ways and in many languages. This is your place, my son. Read, study, learn the tongues; and store up all the knowledge you can hold. This you must do, for even now I sense your destiny. The Church has need of fire such as yours."

The shorn Viking went joyfully to work and the day came swiftly when a papal scroll arrived: *"From this day hence—Rollo, Bishop of Ellenstein."*

Rollo was taken with consternation. He said. "Father—I do not understand. The time has been so short."

Again the abbey smiled. "These are thin and dangerous years for Mother Church. Think not but what His Holiness considered well. You are tied with a silver cord to the Great Heart beating down in Rome."

Later, deep in his joy, Rollo called out, "We'll have one rich treasure here. A golden cross so great that none but a *Norseman* has the strength to carry it. Call all the goldsmiths in!"

And it was done.

AT TWILIGHT, Rollo loved to walk in the cool gardens beside his modest dwelling place. Here he could be alone among the flowers; could marvel at the wonders Heaven wrought upon the earth; could seek to come in rapport with his God.

Upon this night, he stayed quite late, breathing the cool perfumes. Then, suddenly, he sought the abbey out. Found the good cleric in his austere room.

The abbey sprang up all confused to say, "My son, it is not meet that you should come to me. You had but to raise your voice."

Rollo waved an impatient hand. "I would consult you here. Sit down by me."

They sat side by side on the hard iron bed and Rollo spoke: "I seek the counsel of your experience. A strange thing just occurred."

"What thing?"

"I was walking in the garden and it seemed that someone spoke to me."

"Some passerby no doubt."

"Not so. This voice was not a voice, but something more. A wave of consciousness that swept through me in silence and yet it was far more clear than any spoken word."

"A picture printed on the mind?"

"Aye—that."

"Describe the scene."

Rollo's brow was furrowed deep with thought before his words would come. "Strange. It should be a simple thing to do—yet it is not. One thing is clear. I saw a giant ship drawing a tail of fire across the sky. A ship the like of which no man has known. It was coming from some far place beyond the sky and rocketing toward earth like a falling star."

The abbey pursed his lips thoughtfully. "Strange—strange indeed."

"There was a mist far stranger yet that covered it. Or possibly a mist around my mind. At any rate, I sought to judge the thing—to see what lay within—but I could not. It was as if the substance blurred, but the essence stood out crystal clear."

"And that essence—?"

"Was *evil!* So evil that I paled and felt a wave of weakness in my knees. Then, Father, I knew beyond all doubt that I must take my cross and go forth to meet this ship."

The abbey raised a hand and scratched his shaven pate. "The waters here are deep and dangerous. I scarce know what to think."

"The call to go was clear as any call I ever had."

The abbey still stared at the floor.

"You tell me this—confide in me. Now tell me how you want me to reply."

"So I will know if I must go or stay."

THE ELDER man sat silent for a time—then raised his eyes and slowly shook his head. "That, my son, I cannot do. This only may I say: You are the Bishop here—not I. Your hand is in the Hand of God—not mine. It ill behooves a waddling duck to tell an eagle where to fly. The decision must be yours and yours alone."

Rollo sat for a time, sore troubled. Then the abbey said, "But this I tell you. I'll stake my love of truth on your decision whether it's to go or stay."

Rollo got suddenly to his feet. He took the old man's hand. "Thank you, Father. Now I know. I must obey the call. Come you with me to get the golden cross."

"You go alone?"

"I go alone."

"But where?"

Rollo stopped and stood deep in thought. "To the west. To a place where the river bends, then slightly north. I have no fear. I will be led aright."

Still troubled, the abbey said, "But all alone and carrying the cross. It is so large two ordinary men can scarcely lift up its weight."

Rollo laughed. "You forget my heritage. I was a Viking in my wilder days. And in all the *norseland,* only one had greater strength than I."

"And who was he?"

"Rolf of the Golden Horn—God love his mighty heart!"

"And God preserve his soul. Farewell, Rollo, Bishop of Ellenstein. My prayers walk with you."

A few minutes later, an insomnia-ridden townsman glanced through the window of his poor hut to see the Bishop walking up the street. His Grace wore a gold-stitched yellow robe and on his head was the glittering mitre of his office. But stranger still, he carried in his two hands the golden cross no other man could lift.

The townsman spent a moment steeped in indecision. Then he hurried to his pallet to lie down trembling—to pull the ragged blanket over his head.

LALL PACED the confines of her cabin on the Martian space ship as it hurtled through black void. Now and again she stopped to peer out the window. But there was nothing to be seen but pit-blackness.

Even the sun had vanished. At first this phenomenon frightened Lall. But one of her husbands explained that this was to be expected. There was nothing against which it could shine; nothing to refract its rays. This calmed Lall's fears but did nothing to still the hot fires burning within her.

Memories of her Martian triumph helped some. She spent a great deal of the time in recalling details of her vengeance and regretting it could not have been more terrible.

Also, she planned. If this planet they approached was inhabited by intelligent beings, she could have more happy hours. What she had done on Mars had kindled within her a fire, which until now had only smouldered. Nothing in her lifetime had given her such pleasure as she'd gotten from witnessing the vast destruction. There would be more of it. Vengeance upon the whole solar system. The thought thrilled her. Planet after planet swept clean of all life save hers. The whole of known space populated only with the life she herself had created.

The possibility made her dizzy from the suggested scope of its power.

Finally the hour arrived when the spaceship moved into a twilight zone and her pilot husband came to tell her the journey was almost completed. He pointed forward through the window.

"Our planet is only a few thousand miles ahead. I've cut speed. We'll circle it and see what we can find out."

Lall stared at the great globe. It was covered with a peculiar colorless pattern, ranging from white to dark gray. There was much more of the white and the darker hues than the intermediate.

The pilot explained: "The white and very dark indicates the planet is covered mainly with ice and water. The intermediate shades are the land masses."

Lall frowned. "There's very little land, it seems."

"No. The ratio is close to ideal. I'm almost certain the planet is inhabited."

"But by what manner of creatures do you suppose?"

THE PILOT, though a miserable and spineless creature in the hands of Lall, had an average Martian brain, which meant his intelligence far transcended any found on Earth. "I'd say they are not a great deal different from ourselves. Basically, the evolutionary process is the same everywhere. If the higher forms of life can exist at all on a planet, they would develop pretty much the same as on every inhabitable world. The conditions on the planet below should not differ greatly from those on our own world. We are pretty sure to find that the ruling race of creatures stands erect on two legs, has at least two arms and certainly hands with a well developed thumb attached."

Lall was interested. "How do you know these things?"

"Because the things I mentioned are causes, not results. They make the ruling race."

The planet had changed a great deal now as the ship circled it to slip gradually into the atmosphere surrounding it. Now the sun blazed forth and the color spectrum was again in evidence.

After use of an enlarging glass, the pilot reported to Lall: "The planet is inhabited, but not thickly. There are whole continents apparently uninhabited. Portions of other continents have a fairly thick dispersion of life, evidently both human and animal. The population is thickest, of course, in metropolitan areas, and these seem to be most numerous on the coasts of the continents.

"This indicates primitive methods of transportation, most long-distance hauls being made by water. Hence, a backward civilization in early stages of development. I see no sign whatever of aircraft."

"How are the humans built physically?"

"Close observation is not possible at this speed, but from what I can see, they do not differ greatly from ourselves."

Lall pondered this information. The pilot asked, "What are your orders, Lall?"

"We are well armed, but still they may be dangerous. They'd probably try to destroy anything they don't understand, and we could be overwhelmed. Therefore, we'd better select a landing field on the edge of a thinly populated area away from the cities. That will give us an opportunity to get our bearings and plan our future course."

THE PILOT made one more trip around and then cut speed as he flashed over what appeared to be the highest mountain range on the planet. He glided down the far side, over vast stretches of desolate, lonesome country. There he found the twisted course of a river cutting into the western part of the great continent below him to originate in the mountains to the northward.

"I see a likely spot there ahead," the pilot told Lall. "Wide, flat grassland on the bank of the river just by a small island. A snow-capped mountain range protects it on one side. In the other direction are dense forests."

Lall smiled. "Set down the ship. It seems an excellent spot." A look of tenderness was in her eyes. "Forests. Food for my ants—until they find red meat."

The ship came in smoothly under the skilled hand of the giant-headed Martian. He gauged the long, grassland runway to a nicety, bringing the vessel down with the nose tilted at just the right angle, the exhausts mixed to exactly the correct coloring to keep from sending the spaceship end over end.

The job finished, he breathed a sigh of relief and wiped the perspiration from his broad forehead. Lall smiled and rewarded him with a kiss. This, he obviously thought, was reward enough for any man. He raised his eyes to hers and trembled; but she straightened and the softness left her, her mind now encompassed with pressing problems.

The quartzite forward window revealed no dangers as she and her husband gazed out upon the new planet. "Everything seems much the same as we left behind us," the pilot said.

Lall smiled and the spreading of her lips revealed white sharp teeth back in her lovely mouth. "Not quite the same," she said.

"I meant the same as our planet used to be, except the growing things here—the trees and grass—are of a much paler hue."

"That's true. Not nearly so dark as ours."

"I see no signs of either human or animal life."

"We'll never find out standing here. Open the port and run out the ramp."

The pilot obeyed with some hesitation. Steeling his courage—what little of it he had—he led the way down the ramp and became the first Martian to place feet on the soil of Earth. It was to him, however, a dubious honor. He shared with many Martians—except those with completely developed abstract minds—an overabundance of physical cowardice. This base emotion was of course bred out of such Martians as Lork and Pralt. But in the common run of Martian males, those found still clinging to the exaggerated sexual urge were also supercharged with almost child-like timidity.

YET, IN the presence of Lall, the pilot tried valiantly to hide this weakness. He stood on the green grass of the valley with a flash-pistol gripped tightly in his fist. Close to him, Lall stood erect in beauty and arrogance, her head thrown back, hands braced against lovely hips, as she surveyed the valley.

Her other four husbands hung back near the ramp, set to dive into the bowels of the ship at the least sign of danger. Only the fear of earning Lall's contempt had brought them forth at all.

"A likely place," the Ant Queen said.

"Yes, Lall," they echoed.

She laid a hand on the shoulder of her pilot husband. "I think you'd better do a little exploring. Circle around the whole area. See how deep the river is and find out if it can be crossed. See if any creatures are hiding in the trees."

"Yes, Lall," he gulped. Fearful as he was, he would die before letting her sense it, which was, of course, a kind of courage in itself.

He moved forward gingerly, stepping gently as though afraid of disturbing the grass under his feet. He felt a pain, a dull ache in his right hand—and realized it came from the agonized grip with which he enfolded the butt on his pistol.

After some progress downriver, he glanced back and his heart came close up in his throat as he saw that two hundred yards separated him from the safety of be ship. Lall waved a hand. He waved back, glad she could not see the sickly smile on his face. Turning again, he steeled himself. He must go on. The next time he turned to look, the ship was out of sight.

Gradually, as he traveled on, his fears lessened. This seemed an utterly deserted place. And pleasant, too. The air was pleasingly warm; the whispering of the trees in the forest he skirted was a sound of welcome and companionship.

There was a rather heavy drag upon his legs, an increased effort necessary to push one foot in front of the other; but this he understood. The atmosphere on this planet was denser than that on his home planet and the magnetic drag was greater.

But all in all, he suffered no great difficulty, and turned finally to test the depth of the river. At this particular spot it was quite broad and the waters showed no perceptible movement. He put a foot into it, found a bottom of hard sand, and moved out into the stream until the water licked at his belt.

This, he found, was its greatest depth. He waded on, leaning against the slow pull of the current, and stepped finally onto the other bank.

A QUICK spasm of fear shot through him as he realized how broadly he was cut off from the safety of the ship. Then the fear quieted somewhat, but it was with slow and careful steps that he approached the fringe of the forest.

Now it seemed not nearly so friendly and companionable. It was a forbidding wall, remindful of another wall he'd seen on his native planet not too long before. One that went forward tumbling always over itself and leaving no living thing in its path except the wall itself.

But the forest wall stood as in silent contemplation of the great-headed little creature that approached it. The pilot was walking on tiptoe now—carefully—ready to spring and run at an instant's notice. Slowly, he moved in among the trees.

A slight sound to the left hurled him against a tree trunk where he crouched with his pistol poised. The sound was a rattling of dead leaves near another tree. He held his breath, and a moment later the bright, sharp eyes of a small animal were peering up at him.

The creature had a tail larger than itself; a tail of which it seemed inordinately proud. The appendage plummed up behind the creature's small back and stood even higher than the perky head which was now tilted in inquiry.

The little animal made a remark in a questioning tone, but the Martian pilot was at a loss to understand the words. Then, a threatening gesture from its paw set the Martian trembling. Obviously, the little animal could move like lightning. Suppose it was poisonous? In the twinkling of an eye, it could leap forward and sink its teeth in his leg.

The creature was indeed fast of movement. Its tiny paws were shifted so swiftly the eye could not follow them. As if by magic, a second of the creatures appeared and stood beside the first. Blindly, the pilot raised his gun and fired. There was the soft *whirr* of the charge clearing the barrel; the quick, bright, soundless explosion as it hit the target.

The pilot lowered the gun and stared at the hollowed out concavity in the earth where the inquisitive squirrels had stood. They were not there any more. Neither was the grass upon which they stood.

With his fear heightened, the pilot wondered if his act would possibly bring swift reprisal from others of the tiny breed. In his mind was a picture of ten billion ants cleaning off the surface of Mars. What if the forest suddenly became alive with even ten thousand of these outraged little rodents? His gun would be of little value.

As he backed away toward the river, the pilot experienced a grim sense of satisfaction. Regardless of the timidity he knew was a part of him, he'd nonetheless landed upon a strange planet and had defended himself from the first threat to his safety.

The second threat, however, was a far different proposition. He turned after walking backward some hundred feet toward the river and saw this threat looming over him. Now he knew the very essence of terror as the gun hung limply in his paralyzed fingers.

IN A BROAD, pleasant valley in eastern Gaul, a band of some hundred wandering Mongols camped by a blue river to rest themselves and lick their wounds. The battle had occurred not at this place, but further up the river, and the Mongols had moved lower down in order not to camp so near the corpses strewn about.

Night had fallen now and the yellow-skinned warriors squatted about in attitudes of ease. There was talk and hearty gusts of laughter at some kill recounted, some deed of slaughter lived again.

Others there were who sat in silence scowling over wounds received that day. The eyes of these moved often and again to four dark mounds—four heaps of roped-down flesh—that lay all helpless by the Chieftain's tent. And all the warriors marveled, wondering how the chance encounter with four men could have ended up with twenty Mongols rotting on the riverbank.

Three were of yellow hair, giants in stature, from the northern lands. The other, a Nubian scarcely smaller than the other three in muscled girth.

But the Mongols were of a number doubled many times by four and all were mounted well and spoiling for a fight. By the ancient idols! How could four men slash with such abandon, with such power? How could four men afoot—giants withal—form such a front that onslaught after onslaught of a mounted force went down and crawled away on bloody sands?

And then—more strange by far—how could these same four men so suddenly capitulate? Stop fighting? Stand with folded arms? Stand mute and ask defeat? The Mongols shook their heads. Strange indeed were the ways of the blue-eyed men.

AND SORE bewildered also was the *Norseman* Lars. Bound hand and foot he lay beside his fellows also bound. Long had he lain unconscious from a blow across the skull; a blow to send an ox to last oblivion. Lars opened now his eyes and blinked at the darkened sky. "By Tor!" he muttered. "What afterworld is this? Why are the gods not here to welcome me?"

Tazor, the Nubian, spoke, "Gently, my friend. The blow you took upon the head still rings among the hills."

"Seven I slew," Lars said. "Or was it nine or ten? I lost the count." Lars stopped to gather his scattered faculties. "Then—then—by Tor! I mind me now! Rolf ordered meek surrender, or so I thought. From force of habit I threw down my sword. But I must have been in error—"

"No error there." It was Rolf of the Golden Horn who spoke, lying trussed like a fowl beside the helpless Lars. "I gave the order."

Lars strove again to speak; could find no words. Then stated simply: "Reason has long since bade my mind good-bye."

"It was a masterly move, our surrendering."

"Your words but prove the fact of my insanity. I swear I heard you call our groveling masterly."

"Full well I did. Tazor evolved the plot and whispered to me just before we laid our weapons down."

"This fool," Lars said, "will be in your eternal debt if you'll but clarify."

"How many moon turns has it been since last you saw the *fjord?*"

"More than I care to count."

"How long since we left the water and the ship and followed the beating of the wolf paw south?"

"Many," Lars growled. "Crawling like four great bugs across the rocks and up the hills of Gaul. Sometimes I feel I'm doomed to spend my latter days marching forever on beneath the sun."

"Well do you grasp my point. Now mind: We came into this valley and walked with the fall of the river, the wolf paw beating true. Ahead stretch many weary leagues, the only highway through this endless land."

"I listen," Lars returned. "But little do I hear."

"Bear with me. Now—today, there came this eastern horde bearing our way."

"No contradiction there."

"And at what speed! Did you mark the way they thundered on the mounts to eat up leagues like walrus snapping fish?"

"True."

"So, in a blaze of genius seldom duplicated here on earth, it did occur to Tazor they should take us with them at that speed."

"Vaguely I see it now. A master stroke. Glad I am that I have a skull thick enough to survive and enjoy it. But tell me this: How did great Tazor know they would not smash us down and leave us dead to feed the wolves?"

TAZOR answered for himself: "I know the ways of men. They all seek wealth. The four of us in the slave marts of the east would bring enough to fill the coffers of the Chieftain even though the coffers be as large as oil vats."

Lars sighed. "So be it. But I still think there could be found a simpler and less wearing way. Why did we not rout these devils and take four of their horses for ourselves?"

"Did you ever ride a horse?"

"No, but the process looks simplicity itself."

"Far from it. Left to themselves, these spirited animals would throw your bulk beyond the nearer peaks. When you came limping back, they'd be far gone."

"But how can the Mongols make the horses gentle down and let us ride?"

Rolf yawned prodigiously. "That," he said, "is a problem for the Mongols. Now we'd better sleep."

But before he closed his eyes, Rolf looked beyond Lars to the fourth dark pile and asked, "Jorgen? How fares it there with you?"

Jorgen rarely used words. For days on end he spoke not unless spoken to. He said, "I fare quite well, my Chief. Good dreams to you."

"And so to you, faithful Jorgen." Then Rolf slept.

Lars was not so easily satisfied. "Fortunate I am," he grumbled, "to be traveling with such shining strategists? Ere long they'll brilliantly arrange to have me in my grave."

Rolf's breathing was deep and even. And clutched in his good right fist, the wolf paw beat the even, steady rhythm of a heart.

The Mongols were astir before dawn. As he opened his eyes, Rolf saw the night guards already squatting at their food. He watched the stirrings of life come into the wild ferocious band. Those wounded in the battle of the previous day, growled and snarled so all could hear of the soreness of their wounds.

The fires were beaten up and meat thrown on to cook. A hobbling casualty came by and stopped to aim a kick with his good remaining leg at the sleeping Lars. The Viking moved. He opened his eyes to see the Nubian pull himself up to a sitting position.

"Ho, there!" Tazor called. "Food for the prisoners! Else our weight will fall and we'll bring but a pittance in the mart of slaves."

The sour-faced Chieftain of the Mongols considered this, then motioned toward some crouching warriors. With ill grace, they arose and brought a leg of meat to the shackled four. They kicked the Vikings into a haunched-up position and loosed the bonds upon their arms—ropes woven in far India, the toughest known.

ROLF TOOK the leg and tore it in four parts. The prisoners ate. But it was scarce enough and Lars, chewing a final bone, debated asking more. But he held his peace and rubbed the places where the ropes had cut his flesh.

The ropes were soon put back upon their arms and four dancing horses brought from out the pack. The legs of the four potential slaves were loosed and they were forked into the high-backed saddles on the mounts. Then the ropes were tied again beneath the bellies tight and hard.

They took the treatment in complete silence all save Lars, who muttered, "Were this fool beast to catch on fire, 'twould be a sorry day for me indeed."

Soon the troop was ready to move. The Chieftain raised his hand and hoof-beats rose into a thunder. And even though sod was underfoot, a dust-cloud billowed up to meet the rising sun.

The cavalcade moved at a gallop through the hours and the Vikings suffered tortures of the damned. Only the Nubian sat as one at home upon his horse and tried to tell the others how to lessen their own punishment.

"I'd take a thousand spears against my breast, drive devils mad to have my blood, in place of this," Lars said.

Through tight-set teeth, Rolf answered, "Count up the days we gain by this great coup."

"They'll not half total all the blisters on my rump," Lars said, and then went grimly back to the business of suffering.

The sun moved high and still the Mongols made no move to rest. Time passed, and Lars moaned wearily. "The endurance of these yellow men is something to tell one's children of. Do we go on and on 'til only death relieves our agony?"

Forward they went on horses made of iron, tireless. Then, with the sun at quarter-sky, Rolf flashed a look at Lars. "The beat in the wolf paw fades. The time has come to go our separate way."

They had come to a place where the placid river forked; one branch to turn along a mountain range, the other down a widening valley toward the blue and distant plains. The Mongols took the latter course and this—for many—brought on sudden death.

With a Viking cry, Rolf called to Lars, "Now is the time! Avenge your smarting rump!" Rolf took a mighty breath, and with one great flexing of his huge torso, he snapped his bonds like string of brittle silk. A sudden whirlwind was this Viking Chief. One sweeping arm snatched up the sword of a Mongol riding close. An instant later that same Mongol's head bounced bloody on the ground to be kicked here and there by milling hooves. Like a whirling storm of death, Rolf cleared an area around about, then slashed with his sword the bonds that held his legs.

The Mongols rallied swiftly, and swords flashed, but not until Rolf had freed the helpless two. The Nubian, Tazor, was free himself, but not from strength. Rather from stealth he'd used to keep his muscles free when the bonds were fastened on.

IN AN instant Tazor had the weapon of a fallen yellow man. With superb disregard for his own blood, he charged the Mongol horde and cut a gore-stained furrow through their ranks.

Lars, by most happy chance, had gotten back his own great sword from the guard who carried it. He spurned his mount and got his two great feet again upon the ground. Then, with a shout of fiercest joy, he raised the blade above his head and it became a whirling scythe of death.

The Mongols broke and fell away in rank disorder 'til their Chieftain, caught off-guard by the savage suddenness of what had passed, came charging in. He led a deadly wedge of keen-edged blades.

Rolf snatched the shining Viking blade from Lars, dropping the Mongol short-sword he'd acquired, and roared at his companions, "Hold! This devil chief is mine!"

The Mongol thundered in, the great sword flashed. Then, for an instant on the bloody plain, the Mongol chief rode hard on a headless horse. As Rolf's blade came around again the horse went to its knees, following its severed head down to the ground. The Mongol chief pitched forward into the nicely balanced arc of Rolf's red blade. It severed him across, from hip to hip; half of his belt above and half below, his torso dropping off to sit down in the dust, the legs to stay entangled with the horse.

Lars, with the short-sword, waded roaring in, to stop two Mongols, swiftly sending them to whatever hell or heaven they merited. While Tazor, brilliant in his attack, drove back, with Jorgen, one wing of the foe.

Then it was over as the Mongol men, in losing their Chieftain also lost their nerve and broke to flee; on down the valley not to stop 'til Rolf, because of distance, could not say if they were bugs or men.

Grimly the Vikings wiped their swords while Tazor bent to kill the gibbering screaming Mongol chief who lay, still living, on the gutted turf.

Then Tazor moved away, intentions plain, to capture Mongol horses standing by. But Lars called out, "Not one for me! I'll walk though it be twice ten thousand leagues." Jorgen then spoke up too—he of the frugal words to growl, "I'll keep you company. For me the age of speed has not yet come."

Rolf scowled at them, then shrugged. "So be it, black man. We will stretch our legs. The leg was made for walking after all."

Tazor returned to them, and Rolf held up the talisman. "The way," he said, "leads down the nether branch along the mountain range."

LIMPING, THE Vikings took the smaller stream, striving to match the easy strides of Tazor, the Nubian. All day they marched, to stop when the sun went low and set the snares in which, luck willing, they would find enough to breakfast on. Then they lay down and slept.

They arose with the sun and broke their fast on four rabbits eaten raw before they started forward again. Just after high noon, Rolf stopped. With a slight frown, he drew the wolf paw from his belt. As it lay in his palm, there was visible evidence of renewed activity in its pulsing. Under their eyes, its movement increased until it lifted itself and fell to the ground.

"We are close," Rolf said. "We come to the end of our journey." He drew the great-sword from his belt. "Soon an evil god meets destiny."

As his words died away, they turned as one man to see a strange, grotesque form moving toward them. To make it even more unbelievable, the creature, whether human or animal, was coming backwards from a strip of forest. He was of spindly, underfed body and wore a head the like of which no Viking nor Nubian had ever seen. A huge, misshapen head.

The creature backed relentlessly toward them, raising each small foot with great care in its turn, to set it down as though he walked on fragile eggs. As he moved nearer, he gripped some strange instrument in his right hand and stared at the harmless forest as though it were inhabited by devils.

The four stood motion less, overcome by sheer surprise. Now the creature was upon them. He turned and froze. On his face was written such abject terror as to be ludicrous.

Gently, Lars reached out and lifted the thing by its collar. He held it forth and spoke to Rolf: "Is this your evil god?"

Then Lars put it down and surrendered to great laughter. He slapped his thick thighs as the roaring of his merriment echoed through the trees. But only to laugh anew as the creature streaked away, its thin legs flying as it rounded the river bend and disappeared abreast of the island just in sight beyond.

As Lars' laughter died, Rolf slowly shook his head. "No," he said firmly. "That thing may be evil, but it isn't any god. Come."

They moved after it, walking lightly now. Lars' humor vanished as they watched, sharp-eyed, for movement anywhere. None was seen.

Now Rolf stopped suddenly and pointed on ahead. "Look you upon it there," he said. "A ship not built for sea or land. And in that ship sits the evil god!"

ROLLO, ON leaving Ellenstein, walked eastward toward the place the sun would rise. The night hours passed and dawn came softly up to kiss the far-off snow-capped mountain peaks. Morning—and then the sun vaulted the world's rim; and glittered on the great cross Rollo bore.

The way was level and easy, the grasses underfoot soft, as Rollo moved along the riverbank. But mid-morning brought the end of easy paths. The country roughened and the grass grew sparse and thin. Rocky, the land, with scrub growth reaching out to catch his robes and make the going hard.

But not once did Rollo falter until, with the setting sun, he came to a bleak and windswept hill where stood a sorry hut. This dwelling was the meanest of the mean; fashioned of logs with naught but sod to make a roof.

The Viking churchman stood before the door and set his great cross down. He called, "All hail to you within! Rollo of Ellenstein seeks food and a place to lay his head."

He had been watched for a long time in his journey up the hill, and now the dwellers in the hut peered forth. A voice, all whine and snarl did beg: "Go on your way, oh huge one. We are poor. And nothing we have to tempt your appetite. Our board is bare. Our son a cripple—our daughter skinny and unbeautiful. Please leave us in our misery and our want."

Rollo, unruffled, sat himself cross-legged down before the hut. "I pity you for a crippled son, but I do not seek a slave. Your daughter may be thin and hideous, but she has beauty if her heart is pure. And if your food is gone—then come forth to sit here and share mine."

Rollo took from the sack around his waist a giant loaf of bread. He broke it and the malty odor rode the wind into the hut.

"Come forth, I say. I would not sup alone. I want company."

Cringing and filled with fear they came from in the hut. A frightened man and wife; a frightened son; a daughter pale and broken from disease, her eyes upon the bread.

Rollo broke the loaf and held forth pieces, which they snatched. With timid sounds, they stretched their mouths and ate as though they had not broken fast for days. They finished up their bread and picked the fallen flakes up from the ground to eat them also.

AND THEN the husband looked upon the cross. He fingered it, each motion filled with fear. But wonder overcame his fright, and he said, "A strange weapon I have never seen."

Rollo said, "No, my friend. Not strange. Have you never seen a cross before?"

The great-eyed girl spoke up: "There was a time I mind—two snows ago—when a man with a shaven head came by our hut. He had a cross but it was small and made of wood."

"He told you not about his God?"

"Nay. Close on his heels came Vandals filled with wrath. The shaven man went on across the hills. The Vandals stopped to burn our hut. They took our food and left my brother here for dead."

The brother, his fear allayed, picked up a crumb, grinned as he ate it, said, "A stupid lot. We had three hens. Each day they laid three eggs—rare hens indeed. The Vandals killed them all and ate their flesh."

The father spoke: "Your name, huge traveler? Your name and mission here in this bitter land where no man's life or goods is safe?"

"I told you—Rollo of Ellenstein. My mission lies on ahead."

The husband's eyes strayed to the cross. "You come without a guard, and Vandals near. They'd slay you in a trice and take your cross. Such golden treasure will not go far across these hills."

"The Vandals keep you poor?"

"They sweep across these hills like an evil scourge; as constant as the winds in their attentions. Let a man save one loaf of bread, one bag of grain and lo' they tear away the hinges on his door."

Rollo's eyes swept up the hill and down as though gauging the extent and worth of the country. "You have neighbors? There are many of you here?"

"A goodly number when gathered once together in a place. But like the timid field mice, they scatter out and make themselves unseen."

Rollo got to his feet with decision. "Call them together," he said. "Tell them a servant of the Christ is here and would speak to them. Tell them that Rollo of Ellenstein brings hope and love and has great words to speak."

He slept on the bleak hill that night and the following day they came, slowly at first, with timid, faltering footsteps. Then, fascinated by the great golden cross and the man in strange robes who carried it so easily and without fear, they gathered close and listened to his words.

He told them of Jesus, of his life and times; spoke of the mighty force He held in His gentle hands. He told them of the new law this Man brought—not to kill but to help—not to steal but to give. He spoke 'til the sun was high and told each man to take his wife and children to Ellenstein where there would be food for all.

THEN, AS the sun reached its highest point, the Vandals came; over the crest of the hill in a screaming wave, down on the kneeling throng.

With a Viking roar of old, Rollo turned to face them, weaponless, save for the cross he bore. He lifted the cross. "The Church Militant!" he bellowed, and using the great cross as a scythe, he mowed the Vandal men and horses down like an outraged reaper deep in a field of corn.

He tore great holes in the sweeping charge and the Vandals all fell back—as much from wide-eyed consternation as from the bone-crushing slaughter in their ranks. Never before had they seen a warrior such as this—clad in fine robes, crowned with a mitre, swinging the strangest weapon any man had ever seen.

The trembling natives had fallen back like wind-swept leaves before the Vandal ranks had felt the crushing blows of Rollo's cross. Now they stopped to watch the chilling sight. The broken Vandal bodies strewn about the ground. Fierce warriors squalling in pain, whimpering, dragging broken limbs along the grass.

The natives did not run, but they did not advance. They stood and stared.

Now the Vandals formed again and moved with a surer hand into the fray. They centered their force on Rollo and again his great cross swung its deadly arc. But there were many Vandals, and in time they bore him down.

As he fell, Rollo prayed, seeing the natives trembling as they watched, yet not retreating. "Lord, give them the courage they have needed long. Let them realize this barbarous horde is not invincible—that valiant men alone can save their wives and families."

But, as a Vandal saber laid across Rollo's skull, the natives had not moved. Rollo went down, seizing a Vandal chief to slay, even as he fell before the horde.

BOOK THREE
The Ants of Gall

ROLF WAS sore bewildered and distressed. Slowly he walked down the ramp of the Martian ship and back to the waiting group by the river's edge. The strangeness of this affair was in his mind; uncertainty of what he was to do.

When first the ship he'd sighted around the bend, after the craven Martian man had fled, there had been only sureness in his plan. The ship and the evil god. Enter the ship; slay the god; fulfill the orders he'd been given in his dream.

They had approached, the four, warily, down the river toward the ship. Then Rolf held up his hand. "Stay here," he said, "and wait. This is my mission, mine alone. I'll open that devil's box and do the deed though all the hordes of darkness bar my way."

Alone he advanced, sword held in readiness. Wondering, he looked into the huge, black jet tubes that had hurled the ship like flame across the void. This, Rolf mused, must be where the fiery tail comes out. He sought to enter there. His way was barred by soot-caked grates through which he could not pass.

He quit the nether end and circled round the ship and climbed the ramp. The port was closed. He sought to pry it loose with his fighting blade, but so hard was the metal that he scarce made a scratch upon the surface of the plate.

Now he stood back and smote the space ship hard. The pounding echoed up against the hills and Rolf's voice thundered out: "Come forth! Come forth and face the fighting sword of Rolf. This day will mark your doom. This day your blood—O evil god—if blood you have—will spout like fountains from a dozen wounds. Come forth!"

Nothing occurred, and Rolf looked back to where his allies stood upon the grass. Lars with his blade unsheathed, poised to come charging down upon the ship. The Nubian, Tazor, frowning as in doubt, the sunlight shining on his great black bulk. Jorgen, a patient war-horse waiting there for words to send him into life or death. Again Rolf beat upon the port.

Slowly it opened, pushed outward from within, its mighty hinges silent as a grave. Rolf crouched, his sword held tight, poised to cut down the first emerging thing.

But the sword was never raised, the thrust not made. The blade dropped down to hang from Rolf's lax hand. Also his very jaw went lax at sight of what stood there within the door.

A WOMAN—nay, a girl—in scarlet robes; a creature not of evil, but of good. For truly, if this beauteous queen was foul, then nothing was left there that could be good. The grass, the moon, the sun, were loathsome things, if evil lay beneath that scarlet robe.

She had such beauty as he'd never seen. No blemish marked the smooth and rounded limbs. Her hips were slim as starlight and her breasts had such exquisite contour as to set men raving for the touch of them. Her face, a dream of perfect symmetry, full red her lips, teeth even and white as snow. And purity of soul lay in her eyes, reflecting out great innocence, great good.

Rolf said, "Where is the evil god who holds you here?"

"My name is Lall," she replied, smiling, while she looked him over slowly, her eyes traveling upward past his thong-laced legs; hovering there above; then, taking in the span of his shoulders, Lall thought of the great crushing power of those arms. "I am a stranger from another world, hoping to find a welcome here."

"You came alone?"

A languorous wave of her hand indicated her Martian husbands clustered behind her. "Practically alone," she said. She turned to the Martians. "Go about your affairs."

"Yes, Lall," and they scurried away into the bowels of the ship.

Lall stepped back, smiling. "Won't you come in? Perhaps I can show you things you have never seen before."

Rolf considered this. He frowned and glanced again at the three who awaited him. Then he shrugged and followed Lall into the Martian ship and stood in wonder at the things he saw.

And finally they came to Lall's personal chambers. Strange and heady were the perfumes that smote Rolf's nostrils as he followed the ant queen into the rose-draped place. Lall appeared wearied. She stretched her gorgeous body out upon a pastel-shaded lounge. Her arms went out gracefully toward Rolf in a motion that could have been either invitation or a sign of languorous fatigue.

The Viking stood watching her, his bewilderment decreasing not one whit. "You came alone in this metal sky dragon—alone to this world, clear across all the heavens above?"

Lall smiled.

"That I cannot understand. You would need a crew of slaves to make the ship ride true. There would be duties to be done."

"One man who knows his art can guide this cruiser. It is run by instruments, by machinery. It needs only the pilot and the other four to do very simple tasks."

Rolf shook his head. "I feel it could not be done by so few, unless you are truly a goddess. You do not look like one and Tazor the Nubian said you would probably be mortal. Tell me, are you mortal or a goddess?"

"I am mortal." She held out an arm toward him, then arose from her couch and came close. "Feel me," she invited. "Put your hands upon my body and you will discover it is not made of ethereal stuff."

Rolf laid his great hands upon her shoulder and she moved closer, as though from their pressure even when there was no pressure, until she was against him. Then she reached up her hands and drew his head down and kissed him. It was a sensual kiss. Laughing now, she stepped back. "Did that seem the cold kiss of a goddess?"

ROLF HAD no answer on his tongue, and as Lall looked at him, she had a wonder of her own. This huge, magnificent clod, from his own words, did not appear to have arrived by chance. He spoke as one who was at the end of a search, and mouthed words about mortals and goddesses.

Then who had sent him? That superbrain Lork, who lived in a tower back on the planet now stripped? Both he and his student, Pralt, were known to have tremendous telepathic powers. But granted that in their last moments they'd gotten knowledge of her contemplated destination and had sent mental pictures through the void—who on this backward planet had the skill to receive them from so far?

Lall put a carefully guileless light in her eyes and asked, "You seem to come as one on a mission, handsome giant—"

But she got no further as a great suspicion dawned on Rolf. "Hark to this, mortal, goddess, or whatever you may be—I speak as I have always spoken, and you answer me. Even in this one world there are many tongues, and often one man knows not another's meaning. Yet you answer me in my own tongue though you are from a star. Only a goddess could do this." The suspicion within him had heightened, and Lall had a qualm of fear.

"That is only as it appears to you," she said. "I speak the universal language of your thoughts and mine. It may be hard for you to understand just how it's done, but I am sending thoughts to you, after reading in your mind the thoughts you put into words. Your mind interprets my replies in the only way it knows, putting them first into your own native words so they may register."

"That I do not understand, except you say you can read my thoughts." He leaned forward in quick triumph as though he had already scored a point. "If that is your ability, why do you question me for why I came? Why do you not read this in my mind?"

"I cannot reach into your memory. In order to read your thoughts, I must first ask you to bring them forth. If you but think the answers. I will know."

"I'll tell the answers," Rolf replied. "I was sent here through the powers of the witch Hangra; I saw this ship approach the world. And clear my orders came: Go forth and meet the ship. Therein resides an evil god who must be slain."

Lall's fear deepened into chill. The superbrain! Or Pralt, or one of the other students in the tower. They were all dead but they had gotten in a telling blow, Lall's hand trembled at sight of Rolf's fingers closing over the jeweled guard of his great blade. Still, she felt she could handle this naive and simple-minded giant if the entire truth had not been told.

SWIFTLY SHE searched his mind to discover if he knew how to cope with her ants. Possibly even the superbrain had not known this secret—the knowledge of how to guard one's self from their ravenous jaws. In Rolf's mind, Lall found no inkling that the knowledge lay buried there. In fact, she could find even no image of her dreadful children. Rolf, it seemed, did not know of the scourge that had depopulated her planet.

Lall smiled and breathed more easily. After all, her fears had been unfounded. If the superbrain had known the secret, he and his students would not have died so horribly.

"No doubt," she said, "your message was authentic, but it could have become mixed in the sending. It could have been misinterpreted by this Hangra of whom you speak. It is so easy to mistake good for evil. A slight misconception can unjustly brand the deserving as ravenous beasts. Look at me," she said, spreading forth her arms. "Do you trust your senses? If so, do I look evil to you?"

Rolf, sore puzzled, shook his head. "Never in all my time have I seen such beauty—such obvious purity—a heart so clean reflected in two eyes. Tazor, the Nubian, said it could be so—that good could be wrongly adjudged as evil."

"This Tazor. He must be a man of mighty mind. Twice you have spoken of him. Who is he?"

"He is a black man who has always been a slave. But his wisdom is beyond any I have known. He speaks with a level tongue and has watched and listened many years."

"A black man. But you are fair. Tell me—are the men of this planet vari-colored."

"There are yellow men who come with sword and flame from the east. There are black men who mainly serve as slaves. And the white men who overshadow all the rest in skill and courage."

With the need for fear allayed, Lall's own urgent desires, the hot demands of her very nature came to the fore. Again her arms slid over Rolf's shoulders, and her rosebud lips were tilted toward his own.

"A certain white man stirs my blood," she said. "And I could stir within him such fires of love as he has never dreamed."

Rolf drew back from her. "A man would be of stone if his blood did not heat at sight of you. But I am pledged. I've taken me a wife who's yet a virgin waiting in the north. My vows stand like a wall before me now."

Lall stepped back laughing. She smiled up at him like a gorgeous imp. "What are you going to do with me?"

"I do not know. I must seek counsel with Tazor and Lars."

"I will not go away."

Rolf turned toward the exit of the ship. Lall's word held him. "A thought. Why not send to me this Tazor in whom you put such trust? I will talk to him as I have talked to you and he can judge."

"That will be done," Rolf said, and left the perfume of her presence, deep in thought.

ALONE, LALL spent some time also in deep thought. After a while, she stepped to the window and looked out, her eyes calculating as she surveyed Rolf's waiting friends. She pursed her luscious lips and stood with one sharp fingernail tapping her milk-white teeth. Then, as though having made a decision, she went to the door and opened it.

They waited there, her five Martian husbands, and they smiled up at her as one. "I have need of you," she said.

"Yes, Lall."

Or rather—was her unspoken thought—my need for you is over.

"Come one at a time at the usual interval."

"Yes, Lall."

The first husband followed Lall into her cabin and stood waiting. She turned and smiled at him; came close and put her arms around him. He was small, remindful of a child standing against her warm beauty. She felt his trembling body and there was contempt in her face.

This he did not see because, when he raised his eyes, she was smiling again. Gently, she elevated his head and lowered her own while he stood in sweet anticipation of the kiss to come.

It was the kiss of death.

Her beautiful lips opened as they approached his throat and the white teeth were revealed in all their terrible sharpness. They settled against the flesh of his throat, gently at first, as though to make betrayal the more agonizing.

Then they slashed in and through, meeting deep under the veins that carried his life-blood. At the same moment one of her arms held his small body helpless while her other hand stifled his scream. Soon he ceased struggling and she lowered him away from her body.

As she looked down at him the savage joy within her welled up into her eyes and they were not beautiful, but held the cold ferocity of a soulless insect.

One by one she slew her husbands until they were a pile of prospective carrion behind the bed. Then, when it was over, she suffered the exhaustion that was sure to come from such violent pleasure of the emotions. She sank down upon her lounge and lay still, and in a few minutes all her beauty came back until she looked for all the world like a girl weary of doing good for others.

It occurred to her as she lay thus that she had cut off her escape from this new planet. Her pilot was dead—the second in the heap behind the bed. This, however, failed to disturb her greatly. Her mind was too full of tired ecstasy at having vented the cruelty, which was a part of her nature.

Languidly she glanced toward the bed. One tiny foot was in sight, bent at an odd angle. She would have to do something about those bodies, Lall thought. But not right away. Not this minute.

She lay with her mind full of the four giants of this new planet. She thrilled from thinking of what lay ahead.

SO ROLF was sore bewildered as he left the alien ship. He crossed the intervening space to the three who awaited him and Lars spoke up.

"I see no blood upon your blade. But I saw the comely wench who greeted you. She seemed out of place among the evil ones that ride that ship."

Rolf sank to the ground with his legs crossed. This was a signal for the rest to do the same. They sat in council thus and Rolf scowled hard.

"It looks Tazor, as though your words were wise. I fear the source of my orders gotten in the dream was controlled by jokers, liars, or other evil ones. Were I to slay that girl, I could not face the wife who waits for me."

Lars looked ruefully at his worn boots and leggings. "You're telling us we walked an idiot's road? That now we've come these weary leagues, there's no one here to slay?"

"This girl has with her several of the stunted creatures such as him we collared near the bend. And no one else."

"I could have stayed at hone," Lars growled, "stamped on a dozen sand crabs, and rated myself as highly as coming here to snap the life from those small monstrosities."

Tazor had not spoken. He sat quietly as though waiting for a definite word from Rolf. The Viking leader said, "Why don't you go as I went, Nubian—into the ship—and speak with this red-gowned lass? With your great knowledge, your experience, some word or sign might clear the clouded way."

"That is your wish?"

"It is my wish, but not an order, friend. At times you seem to slip back into other days and rate yourself a slave."

The Nubian arose. "Though I am free, your wish, and any wish of those I love, will send me even to the gates of hell."

"Well spoken, black man," Lars commended him, "and here's a wish from me: Inquire of the lass if in her ship she has by chance a piece of northern cheese. As things now stand, I'd kill ten men for just one whiff of mouldy *Ballocraz.*"

TAZOR MOVED slowly from the group and turned his footsteps toward the ship. He went with leisured pace and when he came abreast of it, he stopped.

He laid a hand upon the hull that pierced the depths of void. Leaning close, he studied it with great intensity. He rubbed the surface with his hand, then drawing forth his sword, he beat upon the hull until the metal rang. Then he stood back and marveled that not a mark or scratch appeared upon the hull.

Speaking softly, he said, "The men who made that metal stand supreme above the finest mind this world has ever spawned. The world from whence this spacecraft came must be a wondrous world indeed. My mind cannot conceive its splendor and its wealth."

He circled the ship and stood before the great jet-tubes. He rubbed a finger on their inner surfaces and studied hard the residue that clung. Shaking his head, he rubbed the finger clean upon his belt and sought the space ship's ramp.

The girl stood waiting for him there and—as Rolf had looked—he looked at her. But through far different eyes.

Tazor appraised her differently than Rolf. He granted her the beauty that he saw, but the Nubian had gazed on female charms in more ports and places than all his three companions in a group. He'd seen the vast slave markets in the great cities set like jewels on the shores of the Southern Sea. He'd watched them come in chains and stand upon the block, naked like cattle, for all men to see. He'd heard their charms extolled by bearded auctioneers, even to pitiful details of their skill at pleasing any master whom they served.

And Tazor could not look on beauty now with any reaction save pity for the favored one. For long he'd heard it said: Happy the ugly wench who works the fields and scrubs the bricks rather than serve dark-faced lustful men.

So Lall's lush body was lost on him as he came to the top of the ramp and bowed. "I come to speak with you," he said. "That I may give good counsel to my friend who seeks to know which path his feet must tread."

"Enter," Lall said. "And I can only hope for your intercession with him. I wouldn't care to be killed by mistake. I am utterly defenseless and at your mercy."

TAZOR WENT, as Rolf had gone, into the cabin of the Martian girl. But there were no bodies strewn behind the bed. And subtle, rare perfume lay on the air.

Tazor tested this. He had never known its like before. He looked about the cabin while Lall sat down demurely on the lounge.

"I feel your sense and wisdom are far greater, my lord, than that of the yellow haired giant."

"I am not your lord and the wisdom of my friend is not to be discussed. The point is whether you shall live or die."

"What manner of place is this," Lall cried, "where a defenseless woman is slain on suspicion? Is there no justice here?"

"Very little. But we will do our best to find some in this case."

"You don't question my ability to speak with you," Lall said. "Is this because it does not seem strange to you?"

"It is not difficult to see that you speak with your mind more so than with your lips. The process is known among the wise men of this world."

Lall was ill at ease. This black man had an agility of mind that caused concern. She felt the power of his eyes as they bored into her own. Yet, she told herself, he was a man. And as such was subject to her charms.

She arose and approached him with humility. She knelt before him feeling—from her instinct—that this approach was best. "I put myself upon your mercy," she whispered. "I have come from a far-off place with only good will in my heart. Would you see me slain?"

Tazor made no move to touch her. She extended a timid hand to lay upon his knee. He ignored it.

"You come from among the stars." Tazor said. "Why? Were you exiled?"

"I came of my own free will."

"Fleeing, perhaps, from some crime committed?"

Lall felt a chill upon her spine. "No, my lord." Then she came to her feet and stood before him. "Am I not beautiful? Pleasing to your eyes?"

"The point is not in dispute."

FROWNING SLIGHTLY, Tazor examined her with his eyes. They slid slowly downward from her face while the frown deepened. He studied her breasts, her slim waist, her hips and thighs and legs. He came also to his feet and his hands were upon her while she felt a sudden thrill of hope.

But this soon changed to troubled wonder as he stopped his search and stepped away.

"There is something that eludes me," Tazor said. "Something I cannot grasp. You are like all other women I have known—yet different. I cannot name the difference, yet within me I am sure it is not small."

He walked away, then turned suddenly and asked, "How are you different, wench?"

Lall sobbed as she lowered her head—sobbed like a beaten child, and said, "I am not different from the rest.

Why do you think I am? I breathe—I live—I love. Is there no kindness in you, black man?"

"Far more, I think, than you will find elsewhere. But this is not a time for kindness, maid. This is a time for knowledge, and instinct. Yet both now do me ill. You're different, yet I cannot say just how."

Lall was no longer frightened. She felt she had passed the crisis in this interview. She knew full well this Nubian would never lie within her bed. But that was not too great a loss, she thought. In one of the yellow-heads she'd find a mate.

But she wanted to get away from his keen brain, his brilliant eyes. Again she sobbed and stood with lowered head. "I tire now. Please go and carry whatever counsel you will to your friend. If I must die, so be it. But now I would rest."

Heavy with thought, the Nubian went out; and down the ramp and back across the grass. They waited as before, both Rolf and Lars alert to hear the first words Tazor spoke.

But Jorgen seemed a thousand miles away within his mind. His eyes were on the ship, and he scarce heard Rolf's growling words: "I'm waiting, black man—speak."

The Nubian said, "I feel that I have failed you. There is little I can say. I saw the wench and looked into her eyes. I questioned her and sought to probe her soul but I could not. She has the breath of purity—and yet..."

"Yet what?"

"I sense an evil there so thick and black that hell's dark corridors would shrink away from contact with it."

LARS GOT to his feet and drew his blade. "All this deep talk is quite beyond my simple nature. I say kill the wench. If not that, I will stalk those forests there and bring back food. Or could we take food from the wench?"

Tazor shook his head. "I'd vote against that move. I'd not care to fill my stomach with what I sense within that ship."

Lars snorted. "It's old women we've become. Four strong men squatting here—debating whether we should kill a maid. We've all developed softness in the guts. Perhaps a little meat is what we need."

Tazor did not appear to have heard him. The black man was weighted down with a vast problem. "I feel that something happened there while I talked with her. Something that told me what I wished to know. Yet I was far too thick of skull to see."

Both Rolf and Tazor watched idly as Lars went striding into the forest.

"It keeps eluding me," Tazor went on. "I must relive the scene and find the flaw."

"And I would walk away to be alone," Rolf said. "I'm wearied sore—my spirits deep and dark. What fools we be, Tazor, you and I. While we sit out here pulling on our beards, the maid, if she be evil, will charge the fires in her ship and flyaway."

Tazor shook his head. "She will not leave. The maiden fears us not. She welcomed us and seeks something that we have. But I know not what. Let's wrestle with our problem through the night and see what sunrise brings. The maiden will not leave."

Rolf got to his feet and moved off toward the river. Tazor sat motionless as did Jorgen, and the sun sank in the west.

Then Lars came striding forth from the trees with a great shout and a buck across his shoulders. As darkness fell, a fire roared upon the shore and the Vikings ate.

LATER, THE fire fell to glowing embers and they lay as though in sleep. But Rolf slept not 'til hours had passed, and it was thus with Tazor. "There was something," he kept muttering, "something to prove the feeling in my heart."

Soon the measured snoring of the unburdened Lars found companionship in the even tones of the sleeping Rolf and Tazor. Of the four, only Jorgen remained awake.

Now he arose softly and moved like a huge shadow toward the space ship.

JORGEN'S MIND was such as to move always in one channel. Never was there more than a single thought held therein at a single time. Never more than one course of direct action. As he approached the ship, the thought flaming in his mind was of Lall. He had seen her standing twice in the ship's entrance when she'd waited for Rolf and Tazor to come up the ramp, and her beauty smote him like a blow.

In the wanderings of the Vikings through the Southern Sea, Jorgen had never been one to carouse and wench for the sake of filling idle time. Many a southern beauty he'd passed up with scarce a look because no spark was kindled within him. But when one struck his fancy, he moved upon her with a singleness of purpose that was terrible in its finality.

Thus he moved now, up the ramp of the space ship to beat a fist on the metal door. There was no response and he beat once again. Slowly the panel moved inward and in the frame of strange illumination from within, stood Lall.

Jorgen spoke no words. He stepped through the doorway, lowering his huge head to get inside. He spoke no word, but his demand was in his face and in his eyes. The maid took a backward step, unhurried, and he followed on as she—also silent—took another step and another.

It did not occur to Jorgen that he was being led. Nor did he think to notice what her reactions were. He cared not a whit for anything but the fact that she was slim and desirable and beautiful and that she'd struck a spark from the hard core of his being.

They went through another door now and there was no fear on the maiden's face. And even Jorgen had the grace to be surprised when finally she smiled and held forth her arms.

To Jorgen, whirled along on the crest of man's most elemental task, there were only conscious highlights in his mind. The knowledge that here indeed was a worthy foe in the eternal battle between man and woman. Her slimness was a deception for she rode up to him with all the ardor of one bathed in the same fire that consumed the huge Viking.

Here was no shrinking lily—unless perhaps a tiger lily with a fierce desire to meet his own. She sought no gentleness and even mighty Jorgen was amazed at the ferocity with which she met his own—to blend it all in one ferocity that mixed and melted in together to be one.

When it was done, Jorgen felt with dull wonder, an exhaustion he had never known before. It was as though a portion of his life sap had been withdrawn from out his veins. He stumbled from the cabin without a backward look. He pushed his way from out the ship and down the ramp, returning again to his fellows where he dropped upon the sod and closed his eyes. As he drifted into sleep, a sweet and warming thought was in his mind—a memory: She was a worthy wench. A worthy wench indeed.

THE VIKINGS and the Nubian arose at dawn to eat again. They took the cold meat in their hands and tore it with their teeth.

And it was now that Tazor stopped with suddenness and smote his thigh. "I know," he said. "I know at last. God sell me to the devil for a fool! All night I sought the key that was before my eyes and I saw it not."

Rolf put his own food down. "What do you know?"

"That she is evil—that the maiden must be slain. The voice that spoke to you was filled with truth. A scourge of some variety now sits upon our world. She must be slain."

Lars snorted as he went on with his breakfast. There was no occasion important enough to make him lose his interest in his food. "At least someone is finally sure of something around here. That's indeed a novel situation. But tell me—how did you arrive at your conclusion?"

"When I talked to the maid I spoke some bitter words and her body was torn by sobs."

"She wept?"

"No. That was it. She did not weep. Her eyes were dry and yet she made the motions showing grief. No tears came to her eyes and that's the key. The maiden cannot cry! Therefore, she is not human. She is evil and must die."

"This is conclusive?" Rolf asked.

"Beyond all doubt. The devil never cries. The evil are incapable of tears."

Rolf came to his feet with a lunge and bared his blade. "Then I can do this thing and get it done. It will take but a moment, then we start immediately back to the northland, back to my waiting bride."

He strode toward the ship with purpose etched in every bone and muscle of his build. He climbed the ramp and the flat of his sword rang loud upon the metal.

"Come out, evil goddess! Open the panel, Lall or whatever it was some foul mother named you. You've reached the end. But death that's short and painless is a gift when death becomes the order of the day. Come out!"

There was no response. The door remained closed while Rolf's sword rang again upon its surface. The other Vikings and the Nubian came up and Lars spoke out: "I call that rather dunderheaded, friend. Devil or god—evil or good—the nature's still the same. And few will step forth lamb-like at an invitation to their own death. I'd rate the maid a fool if she opened now."

ROLF'S EYES were blazing with righteous and fanatical anger.

"One does not cavil or deceive in dealing with foul things! One speaks the word of truth to shame the lie. Now that she has not come, I'll take this ship asunder piece by piece. I'll drag her forth."

Lars stood with hands on his hips surveying the hull. "You may be strong," he said. "The mightiest in all the northland, but I'll vow you've met your match."

Rolf hurled himself against the door, only to be hurled backward like a straw. He advanced again, roaring a Viking oath, but the door to the ship fit snugly in the hull and there was not an opening into which even a needle could be thrust.

In monumental rage, Rolf leaped upon the ground and tore the ramp itself from off its mooring. He slammed the metal slab against the hull with a sound that could be heard a mile around. But no impression did he make upon the hull. Not so much as a tiny mark to show where he had laid the metal on.

He turned and threw the ramp away from him, doubled his mighty fists and shook them at the sky. "I have not failed," he roared. "By Tor, I have not failed! I'll have her out though hell stands in my path!"

As Rolf spoke, Lall came to the window of the ship and looked out at them. It was a strange look as though Lall had been far away and had no idea what was transpiring. Her face was not now beautiful with youth, but drawn and worn as from a long and bitter period of labor, pain and woe.

She looked out at them and smiled and Tazor was sharply struck by her expression. "Could I be wrong?" he muttered to himself. "She looks for all the world like good itself. Like a mother—deep and wondrous eyes she has. Filled with compassion for all the helpless of the land. Could I be wrong?"

Rolf waved his sword aloft and shouted judgement on her head. But her manner was as one who had been given gentle greetings by a friend. She smiled and withdrew. And the smile was like a benediction, blessing all.

Tazor saw and marveled but, to mock his conscious mind, there came a coldness in his loins to rise and spread like unseen reptiles crawling over him. He shuddered, and beneath the warming sun the sweat upon his brow was cold as ice.

Rolf had gone to the rear of the ship and was tearing with maniacal rage at the grates in the jet-tubes. But the grates held firm and it dawned with sharpest clarity on Rolf that the Martian known as Lall was tight and safe within her metal walls; that he was like a bug with broken wings assaulting the Alexandrian gates.

He fell to one knee, drooping, dejected, then came erect again. "All is not lost! If I cannot enter in and slay the witch, I'll slay her from without!"

HE RAN forthwith to the timbered line and returned at a killing pace, dragging behind him a tree that would have taxed the strength of five men.

Tazor and Lars stood back and watched. "He means to burn her out—to roast her alive," Lars said.

"Aye," the Nubian returned.

"But will she not escape? Will she not set those rosy tails a-flaming and ride them off into the sky?"

Tazor scowled and studied the terrain. "I have a feeling she cannot. I hadn't thought of it before, but I feel that she is trapped upon the ground. I doubt if even that great ship can tilt upon its tail and go straight up. It would surely need some room to get its speed-like the great web-footed birds I've seen in southern swamplands. I doubt the ship has room to rise again."

Now Rolf, with untiring energy, had heaped great logs of wood about the ship until it seemed to sit like some huge sacrifice upon a funeral pyre.

The sun was lowering when he had finished with his self-appointed task. He stood back and called to Jorgen:

"Bring an ember here. Bring fire that we may see a devil roast!"

Some minutes later, the first flames crackled as the fire came alive, to brighten and set its teeth into the waiting wood. The Vikings and the Nubian stood back and saw the flames grow strong and leap about the ship and give the coming night a crimson gown.

The licking fingers crawled about the ship to leap higher and higher until they reached the level of the windows up above. And as they watched, the face of Lall appeared once more. Lit by the outside flames, it was a face of arresting beauty once again. Gone was the pain and vestiges of sorrow in her eyes. She looked with childlike curiosity upon the fire leaping at the ship.

And then she laughed.

But not with any spite; more a laugh of happiness and wonder at it all. Then the merriment was gone and she turned away from the window to be seen no more that night.

But Rolf, with superhuman energy, kept feeding up the flames all through the night. Asking no aid he worked as one possessed; worked as the only man upon the earth, ignoring all the others in his dogged energies.

All night he kept the flames alive and leaping high. No more was Lall's face seen the windows blank with that odd glow of light created in the ship.

WITH DAWN, Rolf gave off laboring and let the fires die. He said to his companions, "She must have met her fate. Preferring to die inside, rather than come forth and taste the justice of my sword."

Lars said nothing. Only the Nubian had a word: "That would take will power far beyond the average mortal man. The agony of dying from slow heat would drive the bravest out."

They watched the flames smoke and die and the hull of the flying ship was black from soot and ashes all around. Now they advanced and Tazor laid his hand upon the hull.

"It is not even warm," he said. "I thought as much. A metal able to withstand the heat and cold of space, would hardly suffer from our poor attempts."

He brought his hand away and on it was the soot-ash. Where his flesh had touched, the metal of the ship showed bright and cool and unmarred as before.

At that moment they looked upward, their eyes caught by movement in the window. Lall looked, slanting her eyes downward the better to see them.

Again she had changed. She was brighter, harder, more brittle. The beauty in her face was the beauty of a fine art piece moulded in precious metal by a genius cold of blood and without a soul.

I can see it now, Tazor thought. The evil in her. Never a face so fair to serve as mask before a heart so black. We waited, in our justice, far too long. It was this justice that defeated us.

Rolf raised a giant fist. "Come out, you devil's thing! Come out and go back to your evil father with one clean thing about you—the trust of a two-edged sword straight through your heart."

"You make it sound so inviting," Lars said. "I'm sure she'll strain herself in getting to the ground."

Lall looked down upon them and she was not smiling now. Her eyes were full of such a hate as scarce two eyes could hold. Her lips drew back from teeth now turned to fangs by the grimace. Her hands came up, the fingers arched to claws, each with a crimson nail of sharpest point. She spoke and though the space ship walls were thick, her words came clear—as thoughts—into their minds.

"Stare! Talk, and wave your arms, you two-legged carrion piles. It's well for you that being stupid you do not know your fate. My children have been born and now are growing up. More will be born, and more and more. Soon I'll see you as screaming, gibbering senseless things, alive only with pain. Lall's revenge will visit soon for the indignities you've heaped upon me. You have not long to wait."

With that she was gone and the warriors looked at one another. Lars was the first to speak: "I'd swear I heard the wench talking and yet those walls stand up to fire and are not harmed."

Tazor said, "If we could have but known before."

Rolf's face was dark. "I will not leave this place though I grow old. I'll not depart without my mission filled. Someday, somehow, she must come out. I will be waiting here."

He turned and strode back to where the encampment had been made. Soon the other three followed and gloom hung heavy over them.

Came night, then followed by another day. Another day and night until a week had passed and Lars was sore distressed. "It's well and good to have a mission, Rolf. But you also have a wife who waits for you. Will you die here staring at that cursed ship?"

"My mission will be filled," Rolf answered doggedly.

Tazor seemed less affected than the rest. He wandered in the woods and seemed at home. He spent long hours communing with his thoughts and was content. Often he was dreamily wont to say, "I love this freedom."

Jorgen remained the mute he'd always been. He stalked for game and set the rabbit snares. But now and often he would stop to eye the ship with something in his face akin to pain. As though a sickness dwelt within his heart.

Then came a day they sat before their food when the Nubian looked up. He laid his deer haunch down and spoke as quietly as though but to commend the shining sun. "The door is opening," he said.

SLOWLY THE door of the space ship swung out away from the hull. It had been a long wait, and the four were held by surprise that this sudden change in things should come about.

They sat staring, all but Rolf. The Viking chief stared also, but he came unconsciously to his feet and drew his sword without knowledge of the act. But the necessary spark of command did not go from his brain to set his legs in action.

There was nothing to see at first, save the dark opening in the hull. They waited for sight of the lovely creature within, but she did not appear.

Then the spell was broken, and with a great shout, Rolf charged from the river's edge straight toward the ship. But only half the distance did he cover before he stopped again to stand as frozen as some Roman statue carved of stone.

From out the ship now came a sudden gush of stark insanity. It was as if the entrance had become the mouth of some obscene river.

Ants.

Ants by the dozens—hundreds—thousands spewing forth over each other, down the hull of the ship. But ants the like of which no mortal man had ever seen before. Fully a foot in length they were, and even from the riverbank the three still-seated warriors saw them well. Six-legged, sized in body as a smallish dog, each ant had a pair of vicious mandibles. These they snapped continually to make a sound like the snapping of bones; a sound that increased as the savage horde poured forth.

The Nubian crossed himself and moaned, "Great heaven what is this? An evil such as no man could conceive. She is a goddess, or a devil, or a fiend."

Lars said nothing. His mouth hung open and his eyes bulged out until it seemed a breath of air would knock them to the ground.

Jorgen sat like one who'd passed through hell.

At first the ant horde seemed to come haphazardly from the ship. As in a sudden spasm of first-freedom, they poured in all directions on the ship and round about; turned the hull black with moving, twisting mass. They raised their heads as though to scent the wind and waking demons stretched within their eyes.

THEN, AS though from some unseen command; as from a word passed lightly on the wind—they stiffened. For a moment each was deathly still. The mass was frozen there upon the ship. But only for a moment; now it moved. The movement made the mass a complete and living thing with each ant just one cell of a monster hideous beyond all dreams.

One omnipresent brain was leading them—this point came clear—as they moved with great precision in an arc. One horn to left and one to right, they spread with amazing swiftness. And before his limbs became unfrozen, Rolf was trapped, as were his three companions in an arc of moving rottenness, the river hard behind.

Rolf stood as they swept down upon him, rolling like a wave; the vanguard always going under as the ravenous rearward ants swept over them. With scarce a yard to separate him from the wave, Rolf raised his sword and slashed it through their mass. He slew a dozen of the insects, cleaving them asunder, but he could as well have slashed the naked wind.

Almost too late came Tazor's cry to break the spell: "Run, Viking, run! Retreat before you die!"

Rolf turned and fled back to the river's brink and found the Nubian had sprung to leadership.

"There is but one way—a chance," the Nubian said. "If we kill some, the rest may flee from us!"

Into each hand around him he thrust a burning brand from the cooking fire. "Move on them now," he cried, "before they move on us. Be careful lest you slip and fall. It would mean death."

Showing the way by his actions, he rammed with two burning brands to the brink of the moving wave. He thrust the brands into the rolling mass as one would thrust an oar into a wave. The dying insects screamed, somehow, in rage. Or else the sound came from their roasting flesh. A stench rose up and the crest of the black ocean quivered and fell back.

Now the four warriors worked as one along a hard-held line. Thrusting their flaming torches among the insects.

But gladly they seemed to die; for each one that shriveled up and fell, there were two to eat the fried remains—gulp up with ravenous jaws the charred ant-flesh and jump forward toward the flame.

For a time the four held ground, killing the hideous insects by the scores. Then Rolf looked up to see fresh hordes of them pouring from the space ship and he called, "This is futile. When our torches go, we go."

Tazor nodded in grim agreement. "Those jaws are poison. Let one touch you and you're done."

"My torches are almost out," Lars shouted. "It's time to sound retreat! Out to the island first in the riverbed, then down the river! No man can fight these things!"

THEY RETREATED from their war of fire on the ants and hastened to the shore. Then turned to see a deadly, chilling thing. The ants did not pursue. Instead, with diabolical intent, the two horns of the arc advanced in line— to the shore also—and arriving there flung out into the stream, committing suicide that others coming from behind, might use their bodies as a bridge to cross.

In horror stood the rooted warriors, frozen by the ingeniousness of this. "It's like a beast," Lars said in awe. "A single rotten beast with a single brain to guide the way, each ant a deadly part."

With amazing speed the foot-long killers moved across the bridge of bodies, thus to form a living bridge upon the dead and stand silently staring at their prey. It was as though they said, "Your fate is sealed, you will escape us not. Here by this river, ere the high sun sets, we'll have your skin, eyes, flesh, bones."

Now the center of the arc moved down along the shore; again the warriors fled; out through the knee-deep water to the island in the middle of the stream. There they turned to watch and saw the ant-horde overrun the place they'd sat at food. Chilled to the heart by horror, were the Vikings and the Nubian, at sight of how the insects tore the meat. Covering it with their blackness; then the black hummock sank and disappeared as the meat went in the bellies of the ants.

Then came a sound fair sickening to hear. The crunching of the bones. For a moment now, the ants in circling swept away from the eating place and Tazor the Nubian shuddered as he spoke.

"Can I believe my eyes? Nothing—nothing is there that was lying there before. The food gone, not a scrap of flesh or bone in sight. Only clean sand. Food swept away so quickly the eye could hardly follow."

"And the knife," Rolf said in a strangled voice.

"What knife?"

"The hunting blade that I left lying there. Did it escape your eye? The handle was of polished bone, and as the ants fell back, I saw the blade with but a metal haft. The handle made of bone was gone."

SO GREAT was their surprise, the warriors only stared and marveled in sick horror at the sight. They saw that whatever brain controlled the ant had decreed a rest. The insects made no move to drive on in. Instead, with a guard of thousands left to watch and wait, the balance moved away into the woods. Like a plague the like of which no mortal man had seen, they went about their work.

The sound of champing jaws was like the tramp of many horses on a hill. Soon great trees began to fall and over these the insects swarmed and the forest giants—leaf, branch and trunk and root, vanished into their maws to leave bare ground.

"*Great God,*" the Nubian whispered. "Not one single man should live to see this ghastliness on earth. It pounds upon the senses, assaults the gates of reason and is like to drive one mad. See how they eat! All things with any life at all quickly vanish on any spot they tread. A scourge like that could strip the earth right down to rock and soil."

The three Vikings were gazing at the entrance to the ship, forth from which, still, the ants were vomited. But in a lesser volume now 'twas true.

"But where do they come from?" Rolf asked with hanging jaw. "What rotten miracle of evil brings them forth?"

"She spawns them," Tazor said. "Out of her body comes the awful eggs that make this possible. The scourge is here! If that wench does not die, the earth is doomed. The gods who spoke you orders in your dream knew that this horror pended for the world."

"I failed them," Rolf replied. And in his words was a sign of mental agony, which only death it seemed, would finally still. "I failed in duty they did bide in me..."

At this, a strangled shout went up from Jorgen. The others turned and saw upon his face sheer madness brought about by self-contempt. "It was I!" he cried. "It was I who wore the traitor's cloak! I see it now. Hot was my blood for the wench, and in the dead of night I went into the ship and had my way with her. I took her in my arms to bring this on!"

With a terrible cry, he waved aloft his sword and charged across the shallow water toward the shore. Before his friends could move, he reached the wave of insects, struck in frenzy at it with his sword.

Now Lars and Rolf lunged forward to his aid, but only to be held in check by Tazor's arms and Tazor's voice: "It is too late! Stay! You can only sacrifice yourselves."

AND THIS was true. The ants were over Jorgen with such viciousness, he was already down, a black and writhing mass from which one roar of agony arose before the end. Then, as before, the black mound grew smaller, seemed to sink into the ground, and it was gone.

Now did the Nubian prove himself the pillar of strength he really was. Both Rolf and Lars were on their knees, sick with the sight, and Tazor's strong hands on their shoulders solaced them.

"Now is the time to prove a man's a man," he said. "Courage to stand against what we have seen is God's own strength. You must bear up."

Lars was shaken with sobs. "I am not craven. I've faced many a fighting horde." Rolf sobbed, "And so have I. But this! The horror of it turns my bones to milk."

"Now is the time," the black man said, "when a man must have a God; one not of myth, but a mighty God of power toward Whom to raise his feeble arms."

Lars said, "Even great Tor himself would flee before this scourge."

Tazor was on his knees and in his eyes shone a light that was an exaltation of his heart. "There is a God. The one true Son of Him who sits above. A gentle savior preaching peace and yet, Who drove the scourges from the court with whips and told the sea to cease its bellowings. That God I turn to now."

And now a stirring came among the ants as Lall, within the ship, ordered them on anew because she tired of watching the stranded warriors and now thirsted for their final agonies. The ants moved as a body to the shore. The Vikings saw the wave move in from either riverbank. Hurling their bodies out to drown and make a bridge across which living death could walk with ease.

Lars shrugged and forced again—though gray of face—his old, defiant grin. "Make haste with those prayers, friend," he said to Tazor, kneeling by. "Already I can feel the flesh ripped from my bones."

Now, half the placid river was a solid mass of ants. And the water strip around the isle was narrowing as the writhing insect circle pulled in like a noose.

"Commend yourself to Him," the Nubian replied. And in his eyes was only peace, not fear.

Rolf's eyes were on the ship; he gripped his sword. "If I ran full hard—faster than any man had ever run before—then I could make it. I could slay the witch!"

Lars smiled. "Your slaying days are passed. You could not take five steps into that mass. You could not—" Lars stopped and stood there staring down along the river to its bank. He clawed an aimless hand at Rolf, found a shoulder, squeezed, and whispered:

"*Look...*"

The Viking chieftain turned, his eyes directed by Lars' single word.

ALONG THE riverbank marched the strangest figure they had ever seen or ever would again. A giant, yellowed-haired and broad of girth. A Viking truly, from the sight of him, but a Viking fully met with evil days.

His garments were in bloody rags and on his torso and his arms and legs were wounds in such a number they defied all count. His beard was caked and matted, yellow and red; his great chest rose and fell in labored breath.

But his head was high, step firm, his blue eyes clear. And in his hands he held a huge gold cross.

"It's Rollo," they breathed in unison. "Rollo we left in Gaul to take a wife!" Then, Tazor raised his eyes and crossed himself. "My miracle," he said, and bowed again in prayer.

The Bishop Viking out of Ellenstein stopped now to look about and see the sight before him; the ship, the ants, the men in the lessening circle tightly pressed. His nostrils flared and to his placid face there came a look of loathing.

Then the voice of Rolf, and Lars too, calling out, "Go back! Go back! We know not whence you came, but this is death! Leave quickly or this beast will smell you out!"

Rollo paid no heed. Raising his cross, his eyes flaming, he came on. Straight toward the insect ring in lengthened strides he made his way. Full into them he walked.

And the ants attacked him not. Instead, a wave of terror swept their ranks. Invisible, yet tangible it was, the feeling of their panic in the air. A subtle sound arose, of faint, feeble screaming in their ranks. Gone was the order, gone the deadly discipline. The brain had lost its power, and the ants, like frantic things, sought only their escape from something terrible that menaced them.

The outraged Rollo made of his golden cross a flail and beat them in his path while the Vikings stared in wonder from the isle.

And also Lall observed him from the ship. Sick in her heart she saw the Viking go, with swift precision out around the ants, to drive them up and down the river bed into the deeper waters where they drowned by thousands, sank down and were no more.

Lall sobbed. How had he known? Whence had come this man who knew that her ants were sensitive to the subtlest radio waves?

"How could he know," she sobbed, "that emanations from the purest metal—gold—would drive my ants insane with fear? And how could he have this gold? On the planet I destroyed, it was a sacred metal used only for images in the shrines! There, no man carried gold around with him. There was a law, and to violate it meant death. How came he with this gold?"

THUS DID she babble as her own fear rose to stifle her. She feared the death that faced her now. Feared it as her ants had feared the faint, pure aura sent out by the gold.

In a frenzy, Lall rushed to the control room, wishing now for the pilot husband she had slain. "Come back to me," she whined. "Come back and guide the ship."

Madly she pulled and hauled at switches and levers that were mysteries. "I will not die," she moaned. "I have this ship! A child could put it in the air..."

And the warriors, wading knee-deep through the carcasses of ants, saw the great ship shudder, saw the blasts go out from its jet, the fiery tails on which it rode. The ship lunged forward with a heat that seared the ground and melted rock. Then, arcing up, it hurtled toward the sky.

But not for long. Before their startled eyes, it quivered, stood upon its tail, and dived. Down through the sky and toward the mountain range nearby. Hard toward the vertical cliff of a snowy peak.

It hit in a blinding flash, and the sound went out for miles around; the sound of the ship and of the mountain falling down to cover it in a mighty wave of rock and earth that filled the valley, covering the ship forever, or until some future race could hollow out a mile of earth and rock to make a valley there.

LATER, AT rise of sun, there stood three Vikings and a Nubian by the stream. Their stories had been told. Rollo's in an exalted voice of how he'd found a land of beaten people on the way. How he had talked to them of God and how—when he himself was down before the Vandal horde, they'd bared their teeth and fought and had a victory. The word of God had come to make them great.

Then at his feet knelt Tazor with the sun bright on his ebony skin to beg. "Bless me this day, Father. Cleanse my soul and accept my services. Where you go, I will go. I am your shadow now and this day hence."

Rollo, his eyes on Rolf, held forth his hand. "And you, my friend—is your heart still for the northern gods—the shrinking gods who could not save you here?"

Rolf scowled. "I need no gods," he said, and covered the uncertainty within by adding, "I am strong—stronger than you, friend Rollo. In the north, you tried to dry the Golden Horn and failed."

Rollo smiled. "Yes, I failed. But I have gained strength since from Him. Here—lift you my cross…"

ROLF LAID hold of the giant golden symbol of the Man of Galilee. He lifted and a strange light came to his eyes. The great cross did not move. Rolf set himself again and strained until his veins stood out and his heart was fit to burst. He could as well have tried to tear a mountain from its roots. He could not lift the cross.

Rollo raised his hand in benediction and his eyes were misty. "Go," he said, "back to the cold north hills you love so well. Back to the bride who waits for you. I see as in a vision that a day will come and we will meet again. A day when you will lift this cross and walk. The day you see a glorious dawning light. Farewell."

They watched him go—the Nubian in his wake—and all was deathly still. Then Lars said, "It is lonesome here. The time has come to leave. This is a dismal place and our home is far away."

"Yes," said Rolf slowly. "It is lonesome here—and our home is far away."

THE END

If you've enjoyed this book, you will not want to miss these terrific titles...

ARMCHAIR SCI-FI & HORROR DOUBLE NOVELS, $12.95 each

D-71 **THE DEEP END** by Gregory Luce
TO WATCH BY NIGHT by Robert Moore Williams

D-72 **SWORDSMAN OF LOST TERRA** by Poul Anderson
PLANET OF GHOSTS by David V. Reed

D-73 **MOON OF BATTLE** by J. J. Allerton
THE MUTANT WEAPON by Murray Leinster

D-74 **OLD SPACEMEN NEVER DIE!** John Jakes
RETURN TO EARTH by Bryan Berry

D-75 **THE THING FROM UNDERNEATH** by Milton Lesser
OPERATION INTERSTELLAR by George O. Smith

D-76 **THE BURNING WORLD** by Algis Budrys
FOREVER IS TOO LONG by Chester S. Geier

D-77 **THE COSMIC JUNKMAN** by Rog Phillips
THE ULTIMATE WEAPON by John W. Campbell

D-78 **THE TIES OF EARTH** by James H. Schmitz
CUE FOR QUIET by Thomas L. Sherred

D-79 **SECRET OF THE MARTIANS** by Paul W. Fairman
THE VARIABLE MAN by Philip K. Dick

D-80 **THE GREEN GIRL** by Jack Williamson
THE ROBOT PERIL by Don Wilcox

ARMCHAIR SCIENCE FICTION CLASSICS, $12.95 each

C-25 **THE STAR KINGS**
by Edmond Hamilton

C-26 **NOT IN SOLITUDE**
by Kenneth Gantz

C-32 **PROMETHEUS II**
by S. J. Byrne

ARMCHAIR SCI-FI & HORROR GEMS SERIES, $12.95 each

G-7 **SCIENCE FICTION GEMS, Vol. Four**
Jack Sharkey and others

G-8 **HORROR GEMS, Vol. Four**
Seabury Quinn and others

If you've enjoyed this book, you will not want to miss these terrific titles…

If you've enjoyed this book, you will not want to miss these terrific titles...

If you've enjoyed this book, you will not want to miss these terrific titles…

ARMCHAIR SCI-FI & HORROR DOUBLE NOVELS, $12.95 each

MANKIND THROWN BACK TO THE STONE AGE...

What had happened to the human race? In the far off future humanity had been reduced to Stone Age tribes, living in an endless series of tunnels…or burrows as they now called them. They lived in fear of the creatures that had conquered the world ages ago. These creatures were called "the Monsters," and they had reduced humanity's numbers to prehistoric levels and sent the survivors scampering into the darkness. But Mankind lived in hope of someday casting out these subjugators. And from birth, all humans were instilled with a firm belief that the reclaiming of the science of their ancestors was the key to this goal. Only there were a few men who no longer subscribed to this belief, a belief that—over the ages—had festered into a religious fanaticism. And when this awakening to a different way to freedom came to the minds of these men, they chanced the wrath of mankind's tribal hierarchy, thus posing the question: which were Monsters and which were Men?

CAST OF CHARACTERS

ERIC THE ONLY
Being a warrior-initiate, he had only to complete his first Theft to attain full manhood, but fate decided to throw him a curve ball.

THOMAS THE TRAP-SMASHER
He was considered the best band captain in all of mankind. But what of those words he spoke…could it be heresy?

FRANKLIN THE FATHER OF MANY THIEVES
He was the chief of mankind and had sired many sons. He was also a "true believer" in the ancestor-science.

OTTILIE THE OMEN-TELLER
Franklin's first wife—the first lady of all mankind—and she claimed to have the power of foresight over any warrior's destiny.

STEPHEN THE STRONG-ARMED
This warrior was very good with a spear, but not too good at keeping his head when the going got too tough.

SARAH THE SICKNESS-HEALER
She wanted nothing more than to be Eric's first wife, to give birth to his first litter. It's funny how fickle women can often be…

ROY THE RUNNER
This brave young warrior, while a bit hot-headed, was considered the fastest man in the whole of mankind.

THE MEN IN
THE WALLS

By
WILLIAM TENN

ARMCHAIR FICTION
PO Box 4369, Medford, Oregon 97504

*For more information about Armchair Books and products, visit our
website at…*

www.armchairfiction.com

Or email us at…

armchairfiction@yahoo.com

CHAPTER ONE

MANKIND consisted of 128 people.

The sheer population pressure of so vast a horde had long ago filled over a dozen burrows. Bands of the Male Society occupied the outermost four of these interconnected corridors and patrolled it with their full strength, twenty-three young adult males in the prime of courage and alertness. They were stationed there to take the first shock of any danger to Mankind, they and their band captains and the youthful initiates who served them.

Eric the Only was an initiate in this powerful force. Today, he was a student warrior, a fetcher and a carrier for proven, seasoned men. But tomorrow, tomorrow...

This was his birthday. Tomorrow, he would be sent forth to Steal for Mankind. When he returned—and have no fear: Eric was swift, Eric was clever, he would return—off might go the loose loin cloths of boyhood to be replaced by the tight loin straps of a proud Male Society warrior.

He would be free to raise his voice and express his opinions in the Councils of Mankind. He could stare at the women whenever he liked, for as long as he liked, to approach them even—

He found himself wandering to the end of his band's burrow, still carrying the spear he was sharpening for his uncle. There, where a women's burrow began, several members of the Female Society were preparing food stolen from the Monster larder that very day. Each spell had to be performed properly, each incantation said just right, or it would not be fit to eat. It might even be dangerous. Mankind was indeed fortunate: plenty of food, readily available, and women who well understood the magical work of preparing it for human consumption.

And such women—such splendid creatures!

Sarah the Sickness-Healer, for example, with her incredible knowledge of what food was fit and what was unfit, her only garment a cloud of hair that alternately screened and revealed her hips and breasts, the largest in all Mankind. There was a woman for you! Over five litters she had had, two of them of maximum size.

Eric watched as she turned a yellow chunk of food around and around under the glow lamp hanging from the ceiling of the burrow, looking for she only knew what and recognizing it when she found it as she only knew how. A man could really strut with such a mate.

But she was the wife of a bandleader and far, far beyond him. Her daughter, though, Selma the Soft-Skinned, would probably be flattered by his attentions. She still wore her hair in a heavy bun; it would be at least a year before the Female Society would consider her an initiate and allow her to drape it about her nakedness. No, far too young and unimportant for a man on the very verge of warrior status.

Another girl caught his eye. She had been observing him for some time and smiling behind her lashes, behind her demurely set mouth. Harriet the History-Teller, the oldest daughter of Rita the Record-Keeper, who would one day succeed to her mother's office. Now there was a lovely, slender girl, her hair completely unwound in testament to full womanhood and recognized professional status.

ERIC had caught these covert, barely stated smiles from her before; especially in the last few weeks, as the time for his Theft approached. He knew that if he were successful (and he *had* to be successful…don't dare think of anything but success!) she would look with favor on advances from him.

Of course, Harriet was a redhead, and therefore, according to Mankind's traditions, unlucky. She was probably having a hard time finding a mate. But his own mother had been a redhead.

Yes, and his mother had been very unlucky indeed.

Even his father had been infected with her terrible bad luck. Still, Harriet the History-Teller was an important person in the tribe for one her age. Good-looking too. And, above all, she didn't turn away from him. She smiled at him, openly now. He smiled back.

"Look at Eric!" he heard someone call out behind him. "He's already searching for a mate. Hey, Eric! You're not even wearing straps yet. First comes the stealing. *Then* comes the mating."

Eric spun around, bits of fantasy still stuck to his lips.

The group of young men lounging against the wall of his band's burrow was tossing laughter back and forth between them. They were all adults; they had all made their Theft. Socially, they were still his superiors. His only recourse was cold dignity.

"I know that," he began. "There is no mating until—"

"Until never for some people," one of the young men broke in. He rattled his spear in his hand, carelessly, proudly. "After you steal, you still have to convince a woman that you're a man. And some men have to do an awful lot of convincing. An *awful* lot, Eric-O."

The ball of laughter bounced back and forth again, heavier than before. Eric the Only felt his face turn bright red. How dare they remind him of his birth? On this day of all days? Here he was about to prepare himself to go forth and Steal for Mankind...

He dropped the sharpening stone into his pouch and slid his right hand back along his uncle's spear. "At least," he said, slowly and definitely, "at least, my woman will stay convinced, Roy the Runner. She won't be always open to offers from every other man in the tribe."

"You lousy little throwback!" Roy the Runner yelled. He leaped away from the rest of the band and into a crouch facing Eric, his spear tense in one hand. "You're asking for a hole in the belly! My woman's had two litters off me, two big litters. What would you have given her, you dirty singleton?"

"She's had two litters, but not off you," Eric the Only spat, holding his spear out in the guard position. "If you're the father, then the chief's blonde hair is contagious—like measles."

Roy bellowed and jabbed his spear forward. Eric parried it and lunged in his turn. He missed as his opponent leaped to one side. They circled each other, cursing and insulting, eyes only for the point of each other's spears. The other young men had scrambled a distance down the burrow to get out of their way.

A POWERFUL arm suddenly clamped Eric's waist from behind and lifted him off his feet. He was kicked hard, so that he stumbled a half-dozen steps and fell. On his feet in a moment, the spear still in his hand, he whirled, ready to deal with this new opponent. He was mad enough to fight all Mankind.

But not Thomas the Trap-Smasher. No, not that mad.

All the tension drained out of him as he recognized the captain of his band. He couldn't fight Thomas. His uncle. And the greatest of all men. Guiltily, he walked to the niche in the wall where the band's weapons were stacked and slid his uncle's spear into its appointed place.

"What the hell's the matter with you, Roy?" Thomas was asking behind him. "Fighting a duel with an initiate? Where's your band spirit? That's all we need these days, to be cut down from six effectives to five. Save your spear for

Strangers, or—if you feel very brave—for Monsters. But don't show a point in our band's burrow if you know what's good for you, hear me?"

"I wasn't fighting a duel," the Runner mumbled, sheathing his own spear. "The kid got above himself. I was punishing him."

"You punish with the shaft of the spear. And anyway, this is my band and I do the punishing around here. Now move on out, all of you, and get ready for the council. I'll attend to the boy myself."

They went off obediently without looking back. The Trap-Smasher's band was famous for its discipline throughout the length and breadth of Mankind. A proud thing to be a member of it. But to be called a boy in front of the others! A boy, when he was full-grown and ready to begin stealing!

Although, come to think of it, he'd rather be called a boy than a singleton. A boy eventually became a man, but a singleton stayed a singleton forever. He put the problem to his uncle who was at the niche, inspecting the band's reserve pile of spears.

"Isn't it possible—I mean, it is possible, isn't it—that my father had some children by another woman? You told me he was one of the best thieves we ever had."

The captain of the band turned to study him, folding his arms across his chest so that biceps swelled into greatness and power. They glinted in the light of the tiny lantern bound to his forehead, the glow lantern that only fully accredited warriors might wear. After a while, the older man shook his head and said, very gently:

"Eric, Eric, forget about it, boy. He was all of those things and more. Your father was famous. Eric the Storeroom-Stormer we called him, Eric the Laugher at Locks, Eric the Roistering Robber of all Mankind. He taught me everything I know. But he only married once. And if any other woman ever played around with him, she's been careful to keep it a secret. Now dress up those spears. You've let them get all sloppy. Butts together, that's the way, points up and even with each other."

DUTIFULLY, Eric rearranged the bundle of armament that was his responsibility. He turned to his uncle again, now examining the knapsacks and canteens that would be carried on the expedition. "Suppose there had been another woman. My father could have had two, three, even four litters by different women. Extra-large litters too. If we could prove something like that, I wouldn't be a singleton any more. I would not be Eric the Only."

The Trap-Smasher sighed and thought for a moment. Then he pulled the spear from his back sling and took Eric's arm. He drew the youth along the burrow until they stood alone in the very center of it. He looked carefully at the exits at either end, making certain that they were completely alone before giving his reply in an unusually low, guarded voice.

"We'd never be able to prove anything like that. If you don't want to be Eric the Only, if you want to be Eric the something-else, well then, it's up to you. You have to make a good Theft. That's what you should be thinking about all the time now—your Theft. Eric, which category are you going to announce?"

He hadn't thought about it very much. "The usual one I guess. The one that's picked for most initiations. First category."

The older man brought his lips together, looking dissatisfied. "First category. *Food*. Well…"

Eric felt he understood. "You mean, for someone like me—an Only, who's really got to make a name for himself— I ought to announce like a real warrior? I should say I'm going to steal in the second category—Articles Useful to Mankind. Is that what my father would have done?"

"Do you know what your father would have done?"

"No. What?" Eric demanded eagerly.

"He'd have elected the third category. That's what I'd be announcing these days, if I were going through an initiation ceremony. That's what I want you to announce."

"Third category? Monster souvenirs? But no one's elected the third category in I don't know how many auld lang synes. Why should I do it?"

"Because this is more than just an initiation ceremony. It could be the beginning of a new life for all of us."

Eric frowned. What could be more than an initiation ceremony and his attainment of full thieving manhood?

"There are things going on in Mankind, these days," Thomas the Trap-Smasher continued in a strange, urgent voice. "Big things. And you're going to be a part of them. This Theft of yours—if you handle it right, if you do what I tell you, it's likely to blow the lid off everything the chief has been sitting on."

"The *chief?*" Eric felt confused.

He was walking up a strange burrow now without a glow lamp. "What s the chief got to do with my Theft?"

HIS uncle examined both ends of the corridor again. "Eric, what's the most important thing we, or you, or anyone, can do? What is our life all about? What are we here for?"

"That's easy," Eric chuckled. "That's the easiest question there is. A child could answer it:

"Hit back at the Monsters," he quoted. *"Drive them from the planet, if we can, Regain Earth for Mankind, if we can. But above all, hit back at the Monsters. Make them suffer as they've made us suffer. Make them know we're still here, we're still fighting. Hit back at the Monsters."*

"Hit back at the Monsters. Right. Now how have we been doing that?"

Eric the Only stared at his uncle. That wasn't the next question in the catechism. He must have heard incorrectly. His uncle couldn't have made a mistake in such a basic ritual.

"We will do that," he went on in the second reply, his voice sliding into the singsong of childhood lessons, *"by regaining the science and knowhow of our forefathers. Man was once Lord of all Creation; his science and knowhow made him supreme. Science and knowhow is what we need to hit back at the Monsters."*

"Now, Eric," his uncle asked gently. "Please tell me this. What in hell is knowhow?"

That was way off. They were a full corridor's length from the normal progression of the catechism now.

"Knowhow is—knowhow is—" he stumbled over the unfamiliar verbal terrain. "Well, it's what our ancestors knew. And what they did with it, I guess. Knowhow is what you need before you can make hydrogen bombs or economic warfare or guided missiles, any of those really big weapons like our ancestors had."

"Did those weapons do them any good? Against the Monsters, I mean. Did they stop the Monsters?"

Eric looked completely blank for a moment, then brightened.

Oh! He knew the way now. He knew how to get back to the catechism:

"The suddenness of the attack, the—"

"Stop it!" his uncle ordered. "Don't give me any of that garbage! *The suddenness of the attack, the treachery of the Monsters*—does it sound like an explanation to you? Honestly? If our ancestors were really Lords of Creation and had such great weapons, would the Monsters have been able to conquer them? I've led my band on dozens of raids, and I know the value of a surprise attack; but believe me, boy, it's only good for a flash charge and a quick getaway if you're facing a superior force. You can knock somebody down when he doesn't expect it. But if he really has more than you, he won't stay down. Right?"

"I—I guess so. I wouldn't know."

"Well, I know. I know from plenty of battle experience. The thing to remember is that once our ancestors were knocked down, they stayed down. That means their science and knowhow were not so much in the first place. And *that* means—" here he turned his head and looked directly into Eric's eyes—*"that* means the science of our ancestors wasn't worth one good damn against the Monsters, and it wouldn't be worth one good damn to us!"

Eric the Only instantly turned pale. He knew heresy when he heard it.

HIS uncle patted him on the shoulder, drawing a deep breath as if he'd finally spat out something extremely unpleasant. He leaned closer, eyes glittering beneath the forehead glow lamp and his voice dropped to a fierce whisper.

"Eric. When I asked you how we've been hitting back at the Monsters, you told me what we *ought* to do. We haven't been *doing* a single thing to bother them. We don't know how to reconstruct the ancestor-science, we don't have the tools or weapons or knowhow—whatever *that* is—but they wouldn't do us a bit of good even if we had them. Because they failed once. They failed completely and at their best. There's just no point in trying to put them together again."

And now Eric understood. He understood why his uncle had whispered, why there had been so much strain in this conversation. Bloodshed was involved here, bloodshed and death.

"Uncle Thomas," he whispered, in a voice that kept cracking despite his efforts to keep it whole and steady, "how long have you been an Alien-Science man? When did you leave Ancestor-Science?"

Thomas the Trap-Smasher caressed his spear before he answered. He felt for it with a gentle, wandering arm, almost unconsciously, but both of them registered the fact that it was loose and ready. His tremendous body, nude except for the straps about his loins and the light spear-sling on his back, looked as if it were preparing to move instantaneously in any direction.

He stared again from one end of the burrow to the other, his forehead lamp reaching out to the branching darkness of the exits. Eric stared with him. No one was leaning tightly against a wall and listening.

"How long? Since I got to know your father. He was in another band; naturally we hadn't seen much of each other before he married my sister. I'd heard about him, though, everyone in the Male Society had—he was a great thief. But once he became my brother-in-law, I learned a lot from him. I learned about locks, about the latest traps—and I learned about Alien-Science. He'd been an Alien-Science man for years. He converted your mother, and he converted me."

Eric the Only backed away.

"No!" he called out wildly. "Not my father and mother! They were decent people—when they were killed a service was held in their name—they went to add to the science of our ancestors—"

HIS uncle jammed a powerful hand over his mouth.

"Shut up, you damn fool, or you'll finish us both! Of course your parents were decent people. How do you think they were killed? Your mother was with your father out in Monster territory. Have you ever heard of a woman going along with her husband on a Theft? And taking her baby with her? Do you think it was an ordinary robbery of the Monsters? They were Alien-science people, serving their faith as best they could. They died for it."

Eric looked into his uncle's eyes over the hand that covered the lower half of his face. *Alien-science people...serving their faith...do you think it was an ordinary robbery...they died for it!*

He had never realized before how odd it was that his parents had gone to Monster territory together, a man taking his wife and the woman taking her baby!

As he relaxed, his uncle removed the gagging hand. "What kind of Theft was it that my parents died in?"

Thomas examined his face and seemed satisfied. "The kind you're going after," he said. "If you are your father's son. If you're man enough to continue the work he started. Are you?"

Eric started to nod, then found himself shrugging weakly, and finally just hung his head. He didn't know what to say. His uncle—well, his uncle was his model and his leader, and he was strong and wise and crafty. His father—naturally, he wanted to emulate his father and continue whatever work he had started. But this was his initiation ceremony, after all, and there would be enough danger merely in proving his manhood. For his initiation ceremony to take on a task that had destroyed his father, the greatest thief the tribe had ever known, and a heretical, blasphemous task at that...

"I'll try. I don't know if I can."

"You can," his uncle told him heartily. "It's been set up for you. It will be like walking through a dug burrow, Eric. All you have to face through is the council. You'll have to be steady there, no matter what. You tell the chief that you're undertaking the third category."

"But why the third?" Eric asked. "Why does it have to be Monster souvenirs?"

"Because that's what we need. And you stick to it, no matter what pressure they put on you. Remember, an initiate has the right to decide what he's going to steal. A man's first Theft is his own affair."

"But, listen, uncle—"

There was a whistle from the end of the burrow. Thomas the Trap-Smasher nodded in the direction of the signal.

"The council's beginning, boy. We'll talk later, on expedition. Now remember this: stealing from the third category is your own idea, and all your own idea. Forget everything else we've talked about. If you hit any trouble with the chief, I'll be there. I'm your sponsor, after all."

He threw an arm about his confused nephew and walked to the end of the burrow where the other members of the band waited.

CHAPTER TWO

THE tribe had gathered in its central and largest burrow under the great, hanging glow lamps that might be used in this place alone. Except for the few sentinels on duty in the outlying corridors, all of Mankind was here. It was an awesome sight to behold.

On the little hillock known as the Royal Mound, lolled Franklin the Father of Many Thieves, Chieftain of all Mankind. He alone of the cluster of warriors displayed heaviness of belly and flabbiness of arm—for he alone had the privilege of a sedentary life. Beside the sternly muscled bandleaders who formed his immediate background, he looked almost womanly; and yet one of his many titles was simply The Man.

Yes, unquestionably The Man of Mankind was Franklin the Father of Many Thieves. You could tell it from the hushed, respectful attitudes of the subordinate warriors who stood at a distance from the mound. You could tell it from the rippling interest of the women as they stood on the other side of the great burrow, drawn up in the ranks of the Female Society. You could tell it from the nervousness and scorn with which the women were watched by their leader, Ottilie, the Chieftain's First Wife. And finally, you could tell it from the faces of the children, standing in a distant, disorganized bunch. A clear majority of their faces bore an unmistakable resemblance to Franklin's.

Franklin clapped his hands, three evenly spaced, flesh-heavy wallops.

"In the name of our ancestors," he said, "and the science with which they ruled the Earth, I declare this council opened. May it end as one more step in the regaining of their science. Who asked for a council?"

"I did." Thomas the Trap-Smasher moved out of his band and stood before the chief.

Franklin nodded, and went on with the next, formal question:

"And your reason?"

"As a band leader, I call attention to a candidate for manhood. A member of my band, a spear-carrier for the required time, and an accepted apprentice in the Male Society. My nephew, Eric the Only."

As his name was sung out, Eric shook himself. Half on his own volition and half in response to the pushes he received from the other warriors, he stumbled up to his uncle and faced the chief. This, the most important moment of his life, was proving almost too much for him. So many people in one place, accredited and famous warriors, knowledgeable and attractive women, the chief himself, all this after the shattering revelations from his uncle—he was finding it hard to think clearly. And it was vital to think clearly. His responses to the next few questions had to be exactly right.

THE chief was asking the first: "Eric the Only, do you apply for full manhood?"

Eric breathed hard and nodded. "I do."

"As a full man, what will be your value to Mankind?"

"I will steal for Mankind whatever it needs. I will defend Mankind against all outsiders. I will increase the possessions and knowledge of the Female Society so that the Female Society can increase the power and well-being of Mankind."

"And all this you swear to do?"

"And all this I swear to do."

The Chief turned to Eric's uncle. "As his sponsor, do you support his oath and swear that he is to be trusted?"

With just the faintest hint of sarcasm in his voice, Thomas the Trap-Smasher replied: "Yes. I support his oath and swear that he is to be trusted."

There was a rattling moment, the barest second, when the chief's eyes locked with those of the bandleader. With all that was on Eric's mind at the moment, he noticed it. Then the chief looked away and pointed to the women on the other side of the burrow.

"He is accepted as a candidate by the men. Now the women must ask for proof, for only a woman's proof bestows full manhood."

The first part was over. And it hadn't been too bad. Eric turned to face the advancing leaders of the Female Society, Ottilie, the Chieftain's First Wife, in the center. Now came the part that scared him—the women's part.

As was customary at such a moment, his uncle and sponsor left him when the women came forward. Thomas the Trap-Smasher led his band to the warriors grouped about the Throne Mound. There, with their colleagues, they folded their arms across their chests and turned to watch. A man can only give proof of his manhood while he is alone; his friends cannot support him once the women approach.

It was not going to be easy, Eric realized. He had hoped that at least one of his uncle's wives would be among the three examiners. They were both kindly people who liked him and had talked to him much about the mysteries of women's work. But he had drawn a trio of hard-faced females who apparently intended to take him over the full course before they passed him.

Sarah the Sickness-Healer opened the proceedings. She circled him belligerently, hands on hips, her great breasts rolling to and fro like a pair of swollen pendulums, her eyes glittering with scorn.

"Eric the Only," she intoned, and then paused to grin, as if it were a name impossible to believe, "Eric the Singleton, Eric the one and only child of either his mother *or* his father. Your parents almost didn't have enough between them to make a solitary child. Is there enough in you to make a man?"

THERE was a snigger of appreciation from the children in the distance, and it was echoed by a few growling laughs from the vicinity of the Throne Mound. Eric felt his face and neck go red. He would have fought any man to the death for remarks like these. Any man at all. But who could lift his hand to a woman and be allowed to live? Besides, one of the main purposes of this exhibition was to investigate his powers of self-control.

"I think so," he managed to say after a long pause. "And I'm willing to prove it."

"Prove it, then!" the woman snarled. Her right hand, holding a long, sharp-pointed pin, shot to his chest like a flung spear. Eric made his muscles rigid and tried to send his mind away. That, the men had told him, was what you had to do at this moment; it was not you they were hurting, not you at all. You, your mind, your knowledge of self, were in another part of the burrow entirely, watching these painful things being done to someone else.

The pin sank into his chest for a little distance, paused, came out. It probed here, probed there; finally it found a nerve in his upper arm. There, guided by the knowledge of the Sickness-Healer, it bit and clawed at the delicate area until Eric felt he would grind his teeth to powder in the effort not to cry out. His clenched fists twisted agonizingly at the ends of his arms in a paroxysm of protest, but he kept his body still. He didn't cry out; he didn't move away; he didn't raise a hand to protect himself.

Sarah the Sickness-Healer stepped back, and considered him. "There is no man here yet," she said grudgingly. "But perhaps there are the beginnings of one."

He could relax. The physical test was over. There would be another one, much later, after he had completed his theft successfully; but that would be exclusively by men as part of his proud initiation ceremony. Under the circumstances, he knew he would be able to go through it almost gaily.

Meanwhile, the women's physical test was over. That was the important thing for now. In sheer reaction, his body gushed forth sweat, which slid over the bloody cracks in his skin and stung viciously. He felt the water pouring down his back and forced himself not to go limp, prodded his mind into alertness.

"Did that hurt?" he was being asked by Rita, the old crone of a Record-Keeper. There was a solicitous smile on her forty-year old face, but he knew it was a fake. A woman as old as that no longer felt sorry for anybody. She had too many aches and pains and things generally wrong with her to worry about other people's troubles.

"A little," he said. "Not much."

"The Monsters will hurt you much more if they catch you stealing from them, do you know that? They will hurt you much more than we ever could."

"I know. But the stealing is more important than the risk I'm taking. The stealing is the most important thing a man can do."

RITA THE Record-Keeper nodded. "Because you steal things Mankind needs in order to live. You steal things that the Female Society can make into food, clothing and weapons for Mankind, so that Mankind can live and flourish."

He saw the way, saw what was expected of him. "No," he contradicted her. "That's not why we steal. We live on what we steal, but we do not steal just to go on living."

"Why?" she asked blandly, as if she didn't know the answer better than any other member of the tribe. "Why do we steal? What is more important than survival?"

Here it was now. The catechism.

"To hit back at the Monsters," he began. *"To drive them from the planet, if we can. Regain Earth for Mankind, if we can. But, above all, hit back at the Monsters…"*

He ploughed through the long verbal ritual, pausing at the end of each part, so that the Record-Keeper could ask the proper question and initiate the next sequence.

She tried to trip him once. She reversed the order of the fifth and sixth questions. Instead of *"What will we do with the Monsters when we have regained the Earth from them?"* she asked. *"Why can't we use the Monsters' own Alien-Science to fight the Monsters?"*

Carried along by mental habit, Eric was well into the passage beginning *"We will keep them as our ancestors kept all strange animals, in a place called a zoo, or we will drive them into our burrows and force them to live as we have lived,"* before he realized the switch and stopped in confusion. Then he got a grip on himself, sought the right answer in his memory with calmness, as his uncle's wives had schooled him to do, and began again.

"There are three reasons why we cannot ever use Alien-Science," he recited, holding up his hand with the thumb and little finger closed. *"Alien-Science is non-human, Alien-Science is inhuman, Alien-Science is anti-human. First, since it is non-human,"* he closed his forefinger, *"we cannot use it because we can never understand it. And because it is inhuman, we would never want to use it even if we could understand it. And because it is antihuman and can only be used to hurt and damage Mankind, we would not be able to use it so long as*

we remain human ourselves. Alien-Science is the opposite of Ancestor-Science in every way, ugly instead of beautiful, hurtful instead of helpful. When we die, Alien-Science would not bring us to the world of our ancestors, but to another world full of Monsters."

ALL in all, it went very well, despite the trap into which he had almost fallen.

But he couldn't help remembering the conversation with his uncle in the other burrow. As his mouth reeled off the familiar words and concepts, his mind kept wondering how the two fitted together. His uncle was Alien-Science, and, according to his uncle, so had been his parents. Did that make them non-human, inhuman, anti-human?

And what did it make him? He knew his religious duty well: he should at this moment be telling all Mankind about his uncle's horrible secret.

The whole subject was far too complicated for someone with his limited experience.

When he had completed the lengthy catechism, Rita the Record-Keeper said: "And this is what you say about the science of our ancestors. Now we will find out what the science of our ancestors says about you."

She signaled over her shoulder, without turning her head, and two young girls—female apprentices—pulled forward the large record machine, which was the very center of the tribe's religious life. They stepped back, both smiling shyly and encouragingly at Eric the Only.

He knew the smiles meant little more than simple best wishes from apprentices of one sex to apprentices of the other, but even that was quite a bit at the moment. It meant that he was much closer to full status than they. It meant that, in the opinion of unprejudiced, disinterested observers, his examination was proceeding very well indeed.

Singleton, he thought fiercely to himself. *I'll show them what a singleton can do!*

Rita the Record-Keeper turned a knob at the top of the squat machine and it began to hum. She flung her arms up, quiveringly apart, and all, warriors, women, children, apprentices, even the chief himself, all bowed their heads.

"Harken to the words of our ancestors," she chanted. "Watch closely the spectacle of their great achievements. When their end was upon them, and they knew that only we, their descendants, might regain the Earth they had lost, they made this machine for the future generations of Mankind as a guide to the science that once had been and must be again."

The old woman lowered her arms. Simultaneously, heads went up all over the burrow and stared expectantly at the wall opposite the record machine, waiting for the magic message.

"Eric the Only," Rita called, spinning the dial on the left of the machine with one hand and stabbing at it randomly with the forefinger of the other. "This is the sequence in the science of our ancestors that speaks for you alone. This is the appointed vision under which you will live and die."

HE stared at the wall, breathing hard. Now he would find out what his life was to be about—*now!* His uncle's vision at this moment, years ago, had suggested the nickname he came to bear: the Trap-Smasher. At the last initiation ceremony, a youth had called forth a sequence in which two enormous airborne vehicles of the ancestors had collided.

They'd tried to cheer the boy up, but he'd known his fate was upon him. Sure enough, he had been caught by a monster in the middle of his Theft and dashed to pieces against a wall.

Even then, Eric decided, he'd rather have that kind of a sequence than the awful emptiness of a blank vision. When, every once in a while, the machine went on and showed nothing but a blinding white rectangle, the whole tribe knew that the youth being examined had no possibility of manhood in him at all. And the machine was never wrong. A boy who'd drawn a blank vision inevitably became more and more effeminate as he grew older without ever going out on his Theft. He tended to shun the company of warriors and to ask the women for minor tasks to perform. The machine of the ancestors looked at a boy and told exactly what he was and what he would become.

It had been great, that science that had produced this machine, no doubt about it. There was a power source in it that was self-contained, and that was supposed to be like the power behind all things. It would run almost forever, if the machine were not tampered with—although who could dream of tampering with it? In its visions were locked, not only the secrets of every individual human being, but enormous mysteries that the whole of Mankind had to solve before it could work out its salvation through the rituals and powers of the ancestral science.

Now, however, there was only one small part of Mankind that concerned Eric. Himself. His future. He waited, growing more and more tense as the power hum from the machine increased in pitch. And suddenly there was a grunt of awe from the entire burrow of people as a vision was thrown upon the wall.

He hadn't drawn a blank. That was the most important thing. He had been given an authentic ancestral vision.

"Scattergood's does it again!" a voice blared, as the picture projected on the wall showed people coming from all directions, wearing the strange body wrappings of the ancestors. They rushed, men, women, children, from the four corners of the glittering screen to some strange structure in the center and disappeared into its entrance. More and more poured in, more and more kept materializing at the edges and scrambling toward the structure in the center.

"Scattergood's does it again!" the vision yelled out at them. "The sale of sales! The value of values! Only at Scattergood's three stores tomorrow. Binoculars, tape recorders, cameras, all at tremendous reductions, many below cost. Value, value, value!"

Now the vision showed only objects. Strange, unfamiliar objects such as the ancestors used. And as each object appeared, the voice recited a charm over it. Powerful and ancient magic this, the forgotten lore of Ancestor-Science.

"Krafft-Yahrmann Exposure Meters, the best there is, you've heard about them and now you can buy them, the light meter that's an eye-opener, a price to fit every pocketbook, eight dollars and ninety-five cents, tomorrow at Scattergood's, absolutely only one to a customer.

"Kyoto Automatic Eight-Millimeter Movie Cameras with an f 1.4 lens and an electric eye that does all the focusing and gives you a perfect exposure every single time. As low as three dollars a week. The supply is limited, so hurry, hurry, hurry!"

ERIC watched the sequence unfold, his hands squeezing each other, his eyes almost distended in reverence and concentration. This was the clue to his life, to what he might become. This was the sequence that the record machine of the ancestors, turned on at random, had vouchsafed as a prophecy of his future.

All knowledge was in that machine—and no possibility of error.

But Eric was getting worried. The vision was so strange. Sometimes there would be a vision that baffled even the wisest women. And that meant the youth who had called it forth would always be a puzzle, to himself and all of Mankind.

Let it not happen to him! O ancestors, O science, O record machine, let it not happen to him!

Let him only have a clear and definite vision so that his personality could be clear and definite for the rest of his life!

"Our special imported high-power precision binoculars," the voice roared on as a man appeared in the vision and brought one of the strange objects up to his eyes. "If we told you the manufacturer's name, you'd recognize it immediately. 7 x 50, only fourteen dollars and ninety-five cents, with case. 10 x 50, only fifteen dollars and ninety-five cents, with case. You see further, you see clearer, you pay less. You always pay less at Scattergood's. Rock-bottom prices! Skyscraper values! Tomorrow, tomorrow, tomorrow, at Scattergood's annual week-after-Hallowe'en Sale!"

There was a click as the vision went off abruptly to be replaced by a white rectangle on the wall of the burrow. Eric realized that this was all the clue there was to be to his life. What did it mean? Could it be interpreted?

Anxiously, now, he turned to Ottilie, the Chieftain's First Wife. He turned to her as everyone else in Mankind was now turning, Sarah the Sickness-Healer and Rita the Record-Keeper amongst them.

Only Ottilie could read a vision, only short, squat, imperious Ottilie. The Chieftain's First Wife was her title of honor and her latest title, but long before she had acquired that, long before even she had become Head of the Female Society, she had been Ottilie the Augur, Ottilie the Omen-Teller, Ottilie who could walk in her mind from the homey burrow of the present into the dark, labyrinthine corridors of the future, Ottilie who could read signs, Ottilie who could announce portents.

IT WAS as Ottilie the Augur that she could pick out the one new-born babe in a litter of three that had to be destroyed because, in some way or other, it would one day bring death to its people. It was as Ottilie the augur that, upon the death of the old chief, she had chosen Franklin the Father of Many Thieves to take over the leadership of Mankind since he stimulated the most propitious omens. In everything she had been right. And now, once again it was as Ottilie the Augur that she threw her arms over her head and twisted and swayed and moaned as she sought deep inside herself for the meaning of Eric's vision, it was as Ottilie the Augur and not as Ottilie the Chieftain's First Wife, for that she had been only since Franklin had ascended the Throne Mound.

The scratches and holes gouged in his body by Sarah the Sickness-Healer had begun to ache badly, but Eric shrugged off their annoyance. Could his vision be interpreted? And how would it be interpreted?

Whatever Ottilie saw in the vision would stick to him for the rest of his life, much closer than the dried blood upon his arms and legs and chest. How could you possibly interpret such a vision? Eric the Scattergood? That was meaningless. Eric the Value? No, that was a little better, but it was dreadfully vague, almost as bad as a blank vision.

He stared past Ottilie's writhing figure to where his uncle stood, surrounded by his band, a little to the left of the Throne Mound. Thomas the Trap-Smasher was watching Ottilie and grinning with all his teeth.

What did he find so funny, Eric wondered desperately? Was there nothing holy to him? Didn't he realize how important it was to Eric's future that his vision be readable, that he get a name to be proud of? What was funny in Ottilie's agony as she gave birth to Eric's future?

He realized that Ottilie was beginning to make coherent sounds. He strained his ears to listen. This, this was it. Who he really was. Who he would be, for all his life.

"Three times," Ottilie mumbled in a voice that steadily grew clearer and louder, "three times our ancestors gave Eric his name. Three repetitions they made. Three different ways they called on him to become what their science needed him to be. And all of you heard it, and I heard it, and Eric heard it too."

Which, Eric puzzled, which among the many strange magical statements had contained his name and his life's work? He waited for the Augur to come out with it. He had almost given up breathing.

Her body relaxed now, her hands hanging at her sides, Ottilie was speaking to them in a sharp, authoritative voice as she stared at the wall of the burrow where the vision had appeared.

" 'A light meter that's an eye-opener,' the ancestor-science said," she reminded them. "And 'an electric eye that does all the focusing.' And 'you see further, you see clearer, you pay less,' the Record-Machine told us of Eric. What the ancestors want of Eric is unmistakable, what he must be if we are to hit back at the Monsters and regain the Earth which is rightfully ours."

THANK the record machine, thank each and every ancestor! At least the message had been unmistakable. But what precisely had it been?

Ottilie the Augur, the Omen-Teller, turned to face him now where he stood apart from the rest of eagerly watching Mankind. He straightened up and stood stiffly to learn his fate.

"Eric," she said. "Eric the Only, Eric the Singleton, you go out now to make your Theft. If you are successful and return alive, you will become a man. And as a man you will no longer be Eric the Only, you will be Eric the Eye. Eric the Eye, Eric the Espier, Eric who seeks out the path for Mankind. Eric who hits back at the Monsters with his eye, his open eye, his electric eye, his further-seeing, clearer-seeing, less-paying eye. For this is the word of the ancestors, and all of you have heard it."

At last Eric could take a deep breath, and he did so now, noisily, in common with the whole of Mankind who had been hanging on Ottilie's words. Eric the Eye—that was what he was to be. If he was successful...and if he lived.

Eric the Eye. Eric the Espier. Now he knew about himself. It was fixed, and for all time. It was a good name to bear, a fine personality to have. He had been very fortunate.

Rita the Record-Keeper and her daughter, Harriet the History-Teller, rolled the record machine back into its accustomed holy place, the niche in the wall behind the Throne Mound. Despite the sacred quality of the act in which she was engaged, the younger woman could not take her eyes off Eric. He was a person of consequence now, or at least would be when he returned. Other young and mating-aged women, he noticed, were looking at him the same way.

He began to walk around in a little circle before Mankind, and as he walked, he strutted. He waited until Ottilie, no longer the Augur now, no longer the Omen-Teller, but once more the Chieftain's First Wife—he waited until she had returned to her place at the head of the Female Society, before he began to sing.

He threw back his head and spread out his arms and danced proudly, stampingly, before Mankind. He spun around in great dizzying circles and leaped in the air and came down with wrenching spasmodic twists of his legs and arms. And as he danced, he sang.

He sang out of the pride that racked his chest like a soul coughing, out of the majesty of the warrior-that-was-to-be, out of his sure knowledge of self. And he sang his promise to his fellows:

I am Eric the Eye,
Eric the Open Eye,
Eric the Electric Eye,
Eric the Further-Seeing, Clearer-Seeing, Less-Paying Eye.
Eric the Espier—
Eric who finds and points out the way.
Are you lost in a strange place?
I will show you the path to your home.
Does the burrow break off in too many branches?
I will pick out the best one and Mankind shall walk through in safety.
Are there enemies about, hidden traps, unthought-of dangers?
I will see them and give warning of them in time.
I will walk at the head of the line of warriors and see for them,
And they shall be confident and they shall conquer—
For they have Eric the Espier to lead the way and point the path!

SO he sang as he danced before Mankind, under the enormous glow lamps of its great central burrow. He sang of his mission in life as just a few short auld lang synes ago he had heard Roy the Runner, at his initiation, sing of the fleetness and swiftness that he would soon be the master of; as his Uncle Thomas had sung long before that of his coming ability to detect and dismantle traps; as once his own father had sung of the robberies he was to commit, of the storerooms he would empty for the benefit of Mankind. He sang and he leaped and he whirled, and all the while the watching host of Mankind beat time with its feet and hands and played chorus in the litany of his triumph.

Then came a loud grunt from Franklin the Father of Many Thieves. The noise stopped. Eric danced to a quivering halt, his body wet all over, his limbs still trembling.

"That is what is to be," Franklin pointed out, "once the Theft has been made. But first, first comes the Theft. Always before manhood comes the Theft. Now let us speak of your Theft."

"I will go into the very home of the Monsters," Eric announced proudly, his head thrown back before the chief. "I will go into their home alone, with no companion but my own weapons, as a warrior should. I will steal from them, no matter what the danger, no matter what the threat. And what I steal, I will bring back for the use and enjoyment of Mankind."

Franklin nodded and made the formal reply. "That is good, and it is spoken like a warrior. What do you promise to steal from the Monsters? For your first Theft must be a promise made in advance and kept, kept exactly."

Now they were at it. Eric glanced at his uncle for support. Thomas the Trap-Smasher was staring off in a different direction. Eric licked his lips. Well, maybe it wouldn't be too bad. After all, a youth going off on his first Theft had complete freedom of choice.

"I promise to make my theft in the third category," he said, his voice trembling just a little.

The results were much more than he had anticipated. Franklin the Father of Many Thieves yelped sharply. He leaped off the Royal Mound and stood gaping at Eric for a while. His great belly and fat arms quivered with disbelief.

"The third category, did you say? The *third?*"

Eric, thoroughly frightened now, nodded.

Franklin turned to Chief Wife Ottilie. They both peered through the ranks of Mankind to where Thomas the Trap-

Smasher stood in the midst of his band, seemingly unconcerned by the sensation that had just been created.

"What *is* this, Thomas?" the chief demanded, all ceremony and formality gone from his speech. "What are you trying to pull? What's this third category stuff you're up to?"

Thomas the Trap-Smasher turned a bland eye upon him. "What am *I* up to? I'm not up to a damn thing. The boy's got a right to pick his category. If he wants to steal in the third category, well, that's his business. What have I got to do with it?"

The chief stared at him for a few moments longer. Then he swung back to Eric and said shortly: "All right. You've chosen the third category it is. Now let's get on with the feast."

SOMEHOW it was all spoiled for Eric. The initiation feast that preceded a first Theft—how he had looked forward to it! But he was apparently involved in something going on in Mankind, something dangerous and unsavory.

The chief obviously considered him an important factor in whatever difficulty had arisen. Usually, an initiate about to depart on a Theft was the focus of all conversation as Mankind ate in its central burrow, the women squatting on one side, the men on the other, the children at the far ends where light was dim. But at this meal, the chief made only the most necessary ritual remarks to Eric. His eyes kept wandering from him to Thomas the Trap-Smasher.

Once in a while, Franklin's eyes met those of Ottilie, his favored and first wife, across the feast that had been spread the length of the burrow. He seemed to be saying something to her, although neither of them moved their lips. Then they would nod at each other and look back to Eric's uncle.

The rest of Mankind became aware of the strained atmosphere; there was little of the usual laughter and gaiety of an initiation feast. The Trap-Smasher's band had pulled in tightly all around him; most of them were not even bothering to eat but sat watchful and alert. Other band captains—men like Stephen the Strong-Armed and Harold the Hurler—had worried looks on their faces as if they were calculating highly complex problems.

Even the children were remarkably quiet. They served the food over, which the women had said charms much earlier, then scurried to their places and ate with wide eyes aimed at their elders.

All in all, Eric was distinctly relieved when Franklin the Father of Many Thieves belched commandingly, stretched, and lay back on the floor of the burrow. In a few minutes, he was asleep, snoring loudly.

Night had officially begun.

CHAPTER THREE

AT the end of the sleep period, as soon as the chief had awakened and yawned, thus proclaiming the dawn, Thomas the Trap-Smasher's band started on its trip.

Eric, still officially surnamed the Only, carried the precious loin straps of manhood in the food knapsack the women had provided for a possible journey of several days. They should return before the next sleep period, but when one went on an expedition into Monster territory anything might happen.

They stepped out in full military formation, a long, straggling single file, each man barely in sight of the warrior immediately ahead. For the first time in his military career, Eric was wearing only one set of spears—those for himself. Extra weapons for the band—as well as extra supplies—were on the back of a new apprentice, a stripling who marched a distance behind Eric, watching him with the same mixture of fright and exhilaration Eric himself had once accorded all other warriors.

Ahead of Eric, momentarily disappearing as the dim corridor curved and branched, was Roy the Runner, his long, loose-jointed legs purposefully treading down the mileage. And all the way in the lead of the column, Eric knew, was his uncle. Thomas the Trap-Smasher would be striding cautiously yet without any unnecessary waste of time, the large glow lamp on his forehead constantly shifting from wall to wall of the uninhabited burrow and then straight ahead, the heavy spear in each brawny hand ready for instant action, his mouth set to call the warning behind him if danger materialized.

To be a man—this was what it was like! To go on expeditions like this for the rest of one's life, glorious, adventure-charged expeditions so that Mankind might eat well and have weapons and live as Mankind should. And when you returned, triumphant, victorious, the welcoming dance of the women as they threaded their way through the tired ranks, giving you refreshment and taking from you the supplies that only they could turn into usable articles. Then, after you had eaten and drunk and rested, your own dance, the dance of the men, where you sang and acted out for the tribe all the events of this particular expedition, the dangers you had overcome, the splendid courage you had shown the strange and mysterious sights you had seen.

The sights you had seen! As Eric the Eye, he would probably be entitled to a solo dance anytime his band came across anything particularly curious. Oh how high Eric the Eye would leap, how loudly, how proudly, how melodiously, he would sing of the wonders the expedition had encountered!

"Eric the Eye," the women would murmur. "What a fine, fine figure of a man! What a mate for some lucky woman!"

HARRIET the History-Teller this morning, for example, before they started out, she had filled his canteen for him with fresh water as if he were already an accredited man instead of at initiate going out to face his ultimate trial. Before the eyes of all Mankind she had filled it and brought it to him, her eyes downcast and light purple blushes on the rosy skin of her face and body. She had treated him the way a wife treats a husband, and many warriors—Eric thought gleefully—many full warriors with their Thefts long behind them had observed that Eric was likely to join the ranks of the Male Society and the married men almost simultaneously.

Of course, with her unlucky red hair, her bustling, domineering mother, Harriet was not exactly the most marriageable girl in Mankind. Still, there were many full warriors who had not yet been able to persuade a woman to mate with them, who watched Franklin and his three wives with unconcealed hunger and envy. How they would envy Eric, the newest warrior of all, when he mated the same night he returned from his theft! Call him Only, then! Call him singleton, then!

They would have litter after litter, he and Harriet, large litters, ample litters, four, five, even six at a time. People would forget he'd ever been the product of a singleton birth. Other women, mates of other warriors, would wriggle to attract his attention as they now wriggled when they caught the eye of Franklin the Father of Many Thieves. He would make the litters fathered by Franklin look puny in comparison, he would prove that the best hope for Mankind's increase lay in his loins and his loins alone. And when the time came to select another chief...

"Hey, you damned day-dreaming singleton!" Roy the Runner was calling from the burrow ahead. "Will you wipe that haze out of your face and pay attention to signals? This is an expedition to Monster territory, not a stroll in the women's quarters. Stay alert, will you? The band captain's sent down a call for you."

Amid the chuckles ahead and behind him—damn it, even the new apprentice was laughing!—Eric took a firmer grip on his glow torch and sprinted for the head of the column. As he passed each man, he was asked the name of the girl he'd been thinking about and pressed for interesting details. Since he kept his mouth tightly shut, some of the warriors hypothesized out loud. They were painfully close to the truth.

His uncle wasn't much gentler with him. "Eric the *Eye!*" the Trap-Smasher growled. "Eric the Eyebrow, Eric the Closed Eyelash, you'll be known as, if you don't wake up! Now stay abreast of me and try to act like Eric the Eye.

These are dangerous burrows and my vision isn't as sharp as yours. Besides, I have to fill you in on a couple of things." He turned. "Spread out a little farther back there," he called out to the men behind him. "Spread out! You should be a full spear-cast from the backside of the man in front of you. Let me see a real strung-out column with plenty of distance between each warrior."

TO Eric, he muttered, once the maneuver had been completed: "Good. Gives us a chance to talk without everyone in the band hearing us. You can trust my bunch, but still, why take chances?"

Eric nodded, with no idea what he was talking about. His uncle had become slightly odd recently. Well, he was still the best band captain in all Mankind.

They marched along together, the light from the strange glowing substance on Eric's torch and his uncle's forehead spreading a yellowish illumination some hundred feet ahead of them. On either side, underfoot, overhead, were the curved, featureless walls of the burrow. From the center of the corridor, where they marched, the walls looked soft and spongy, but Eric knew what tremendous labor was involved in digging a niche or recess in them. It took several strong men at least two sleep periods to make a niche large enough to hold a handful of Mankind's store of artifacts.

Where had the burrows come from? Some said they had been dug by the ancestors when they had first begun to hit back at the Monsters. Others claimed the burrows had always been there, waiting for Mankind to find them and be comfortable in them.

In all directions the burrows stretched. On and on they went, interminably curving and branching and forking, dark and silent, until human beings stamped into them with glow lamp and glow torch. These particular corridors Eric knew, led to Monster territory. He had been along them many times as a humble spear-carrier when his uncle's band had been dispatched to bring back the necessities of life for Mankind. Other corridors went off to more exotic and even more dangerous places. But were there any places that had no burrows?

What a thought! Even the Monsters lived in burrows, big as they were reputed to be. But there was a legend that Mankind had once lived outside burrows, outside the branching corridors. Then what had they lived in! Just trying to work it out made you dizzy.

They came to a place where the burrow became two burrows each curving away from the other in opposite directions.

"Which one?" his uncle demanded.

Eric unhesitatingly pointed the right.

Thomas the Trap-Smasher nodded. "You have a good memory," he said as he bore in the direction that Eric had indicated. "That's half of being an Eye. The other half is having a feeling, a knack, for the right way to go. You have that too. I've noticed it on every expedition where you've been along. That's what I told those women—Rita, Ottilie— I told them what your name had to be. Eric the Eye, I told them. Find a vision for the kind that corresponds to it."

HE was so shocked that he almost came to a halt. "You picked my name? You told them what kind of vision? That's—that's—I never heard of such a thing!"

His uncle laughed. "It's no different from Ottilie the Omen-Teller making a deal with Franklin to have a vision showing him as the new chief. He gets to be chief, she becomes the Chieftain's First Wife and automatically takes over the Female Society. Religion and politics, they're always mixed up together these days, Eric. We're not living in the old times anymore when Ancestor-science was real and holy and it worked."

"It still works, Ancestor-science, doesn't it?" he pleaded. "Some of the time?"

"Everything works some of the time. Only Alien-science, though, works *all* of the time. It's working for Aliens, for the Monsters. It's got to begin working for us. That's where you come in."

He had to remember that his uncle was an experienced captain, a knowledgeable warrior. Thomas the Trap-Smasher's protection and advice had brought him, a despised singleton, an orphaned child of parents that no one dared even talk about, to his present estate of almost full thieving status. It was very fortunate for him that neither of his uncle's wives had yet produced a son that survived into the initiate years. He still had a lot to learn from this man.

"Now," the Trap-Smasher was saying, his eyes still on the dimly illuminated corridors ahead. "When we get to the Monster burrows, you go in. You go in alone, of course."

Well, of course, Eric thought. What other way was there to make your Theft? The first time you stole for Mankind, you did it all alone, to prove your manhood, your courage, also the amount of personal luck you enjoyed. It was not like a regular band theft—or organized stealing of a large amount of goods that would last Mankind many sleep-periods, almost a tenth of an auld lang syne. In a regular band theft, assigned to each band in rotation, a warrior had to be assured of the luck and skill of the warriors at his side. He had to know that each one of them had made his Theft—and proved himself when completely alone.

Stealing from the Monsters was dangerous enough under the best of conditions. You wanted only the cleverest, bravest, most fortunate warriors along with you.

"Once you're inside, stay close to the wall. Don't look up at first or you're likely to freeze right where you are. Keep your eyes on the wall and move close to it. Move fast."

Nothing new here. Every initiate learned over and over again, before he made his Theft, that it was terribly dangerous to look up when you first entered Monster territory. You had to keep your eyes on the wall and move in the protection of it, the wall touching your shoulder as you ran alongside it. Why this was so, Eric had no idea, but that it was so he had long ago learned to repeat as a fact.

"All right," Thomas the Trap-Smasher went on. "You turn right as you go in. *Right,* do you hear me, Eric? You turn right, without looking up, and run along the wall, letting it brush your shoulder every couple of steps. You run forty, fifty paces, and you come to a great big thing, a structure, that's almost touching the wall. You turn left along that, moving away from the wall, but still not looking up, until you pass an entrance in the structure. You don't go in that first entrance, Eric; you pass it by. About twenty, twenty-five paces further on, there'll be a second entrance, a bigger one. You go in that one."

"I go in that one," Eric repeated carefully, memorizing his uncle's words. He was receiving directions for his Theft, the most important act of his life! Every single thing his uncle told him must be listened to carefully, must not be forgotten.

"You'll be in something that looks like a burrow again, but it'll be darker, at first. The walls will soak up light from your glow lamp. After a while, the burrow will open out into a great big space, a real big and real dark space. You go on in a straight line, looking over your shoulder at the light from the entrance and making sure it's always directly behind you. You'll hit another burrow, a low one this time. Turn right at the first fork as soon as you go in, and there you are."

"Where? Where will I be? What happens then?" Eric demanded eagerly. "How do I make my Theft? Where do I find the third category?"

Thomas the Trap-Smasher seemed to have trouble continuing. Incredible—he was actually nervous! "There'll be a Stranger there. You tell him who you are, your name. He'll do the rest."

THIS time Eric came to a full stop. "A Stranger?" he asked in complete amazement. "Someone who's not of Mankind?"

His uncle grabbed at his arm and pulled him along. "Well, you've seen Strangers before," he said with a weak laugh. "You know there are others in the burrows besides Mankind. You know that, don't you, boy?"

Eric certainly did.

From an early age he had accompanied his uncle and his uncle's band on warfare and trading expeditions to the burrows a bit further back. He knew that the people in these burrows looked down on the people in his, that they were more plentiful than his people, and led richer, safer lives—but he still couldn't help feeling sorry for them.

They were nothing but Strangers, after all. He was a member of Mankind.

It wasn't just that Mankind lived in the front burrows, those closest to the Monster larder. This enormous convenience might be counterbalanced, he would readily admit, by the dangers associated with it—although the constant exposure to dangers and death in every form were part of Mankind's greatness. They were great despite their inferior technology. So what if they were primarily a source of raw materials to the more populous but less hardy burrows in the rear? How long would the weapon-smiths, the potters and tanners and artificers of these burrows be able to go on with their buzzing, noisy industries once Mankind ceased to bring them the basic substances—food, cloth, metal—it had so gloriously stolen from fear-filled Monster territory? No, Mankind was the bravest, greatest, most important people in all the burrows.

But that still wasn't the point of it all.

The point was that you had nothing more to do with Strangers than was absolutely necessary. They were Strangers. You were Mankind. You stayed proudly aloof from them at all times.

Trading with them—well, you traded with them. Mankind needed spear-points and sturdy spear-shifts, knapsacks and loin straps, canteens and cooking vessels. You needed these articles and got them in exchange for heavy backloads of shapeless, unprocessed stuff freshly stolen. Mating with them—well, of course you mated with them. One was always on the lookout for extra women who could add to the knowledge and technical abilities of Mankind. But these women became a well-adjusted part of Mankind once they were stolen, just as Mankind's women were complete outsiders and Strangers the moment they had been carried off by a foreign raiding party. And fighting with them, warring with them—next to stealing from the Monsters, that was the sweetest, most exciting part of a warrior's existence.

You traded with Strangers, coldly, suspiciously, always alert for a better bargain; you stole Stranger women whenever you could, gleefully, proudly, because that diminished them and increased the numbers and well-being of Mankind; and you fought Stranger men whenever there was more to be gained that way than by simple trading—and periodically they came upon you as you lay in your burrow unawares and fought you.

But otherwise, for all normal social purposes, they were taboo. Almost as taboo and not-to-be-related-to as the

Monsters on the other side of Mankind's burrows. When you came upon an individual Stranger wandering apart from his people, you killed him quickly and casually.

You certainly didn't ask him for advice on your Theft.

ERIC was still brooding on the unprecedented nature of his uncle's instructions when they came to the end of their journey, a large, blind alley burrow. There was a line cut deep into the blank wall here, a line that started at the floor, went up almost to the height of a man's head, and then curved down to the floor again.

The door to Monster territory.

Thomas the Trap-Smasher waited for a moment, listening. When his experienced ears had detected no unusual noises in the neighborhood, no hint of danger on the other side, he cupped his hands around his mouth, faced back the way he had come, and softly gave the ululating recognition-call of the band. The four other warriors and the apprentice came up swiftly and grouped themselves about him. Then, at a signal from their leader, all squatted near the door.

They ate first, rapidly and silently, removing from their knapsacks handfuls of food that the women had prepared for them and stuffing their mouths full, the beams from the glow lamps above their eyes darting incessantly back and forth along the arched, empty corridor. This was the place of ultimate, awful danger. This was the place where anything might happen.

Eric ate most sparingly of all as was correct for an initiate about to emerge upon his Theft. He knew he had to keep his springiness of body and watchfulness of mind at their highest possible pitch. He saw his uncle nodding approvingly as he returned the bulk of his food to the knapsack.

The floor vibrated slightly underfoot; there was a regular, rhythmic gurgling. Eric knew that meant they were directly over a length of Monster plumbing; upon his return, before the band started homewards, Thomas the Trap-Smasher would make an opening in the plumbing and they would refill their canteens. The water here, nearest to Monster territory, was always the sweetest and best.

Now his uncle got to his feet and called Roy the Runner to him. While the other warriors watched, tense and still, the two men walked to the curved line and laid their ears against it. Satisfied, finally, they inserted spear points into the door's outline on either side and carefully pried the slab back toward them. They laid it on the floor of the corridor, very gently.

A shimmering blur of pure whiteness appeared where the door had been.

Monster territory. The strange, alien light of Monster territory. Eric had seen many warriors disappear into it to fulfill their manhood tasks. Now it was his turn.

Holding his heavy spear at the ready, Eric's uncle leaned forward into the whiteness. His body twisted as he looked up, down, around, on both sides. He withdrew and came back into the burrow.

"No new traps," he said in a soft voice. "The one I dismantled last expedition is still up there on the wall. It hasn't been repaired. Now Eric, here you go, boy."

Eric rose and walked with him to the doorway, remembering to keep his eyes on the floor. You can't look up, he had been told again and again, not right away, the first time you're in Monster territory. If you do, you freeze, you're lost, you're done for completely.

His uncle checked him carefully and fondly, making certain that his new loin straps were tight, that his knapsack and back-sling were both in the right position on his shoulders. He took a heavy spear from Eric's right hand and replaced it with a light one from the hick-sling. "If you're seen by a Monster," he whispered, "the heavy spear's not worth a damn. You scuttle into the closest hiding-place and throw the light spear as far as you can. The Monster can't distinguish between you and the spear. It will follow the spear."

Eric nodded mechanically, although this too he had been told many times, this too was a lesson he knew by heart. His mouth was so dry! He wished that it weren't unmanly to beg for water at such a moment.

Thomas the Trap-Smasher took his torch from him and slipped a glow lamp about his forehead. Then he pushed him through the doorway. "Go make your Theft, Eric," he whispered. "Come back a man."

CHAPTER FOUR

HE was on the other side. He was in Monster territory. He was surrounded by the strange Monster light, the incredible Monster world. The burrows, Mankind, everything familiar, lay behind him.

Panic rose from his stomach and into his throat like vomit.

Don't look up. Eyes down, eyes down or you're likely to freeze right where you are. Stay close to the well, keep your eyes on the wall and move along it. Turn right and move along the wall. Move fast.

Eric turned. He felt the wall brush his right shoulder. He began to run, keeping his eyes down, touching the wall with his shoulder at regular intervals. He ran as fast as he possibly could, urging his muscles fiercely on. As he ran, he counted the steps to himself.

Twenty paces. Where did the light come from? It was everywhere; it glowed so; it was white, white. *Twenty-five paces. Touch the wall with your shoulder. Don't—above everything—don't wander away from the wall. Thirty paces.* In light like this you had no need of the glow lamp. It was almost too bright to see in. *Thirty-five paces.* The floor was not like a burrow floor. It was flat and very hard. So was the wall. Flat and hard and straight. *Forty paces. Run and keep your eyes down. Run. Keep touching the wall with your shoulder. Move fast. But keep your eyes down. Don't look up. Forty-five paces.*

He almost smashed into the structure he had been told about, but his reflexes and the warnings he had received swung him to the left and along it just in time. It was a different color than the wall, he noted, and a different textured material. *Keep your eyes down. Don't look up.* He came to an entrance, like the beginning of a small burrow.

Don't go in that first entrance, Eric; you pass it by. He began to count again as he ran. Twenty-three paces more, and there was another entrance, a much higher, wider one. He darted inside. *It'll be darker, at first. The walls will soak up light from your glow lamp.*

Eric paused, gasping. He was grateful for the sucking darkness. After that terrible, alien white light, the gloom was friendly, reminiscent of the familiar burrows now so horribly far away.

He could afford to take a breath at this point, he knew. The first, the worst part was over. He wasn't out in the open any more.

He had emerged into Monster territory. He had run fast, following instructions until he was safely under cover again. He was still alive.

The worst was over. Nothing else would be as bad as this.

Monster territory. It lay behind him, bathed in its own peculiar light. Now. Why not? Now, when he was in a place of comparative safety. He could take a chance. He *wanted* to take a chance.

He turned, gingerly, fearfully.

He raised his eyes. He looked.

THE cry that tore from his lips was completely involuntary and frightened him almost as much as what he saw. He shut his eyes and threw himself down and sideways. He lay where he had fallen for a long while, almost paralyzed.

It couldn't be. He hadn't seen it. Nothing was that high, nothing ran on and on for such incredible distances!

After a time, he opened his eyes again, keeping them carefully focused on the dark near him. The gloom in this covered place had diminished somewhat as his eyes had grown more accustomed to it. Yellowish light from his glow lamp was providing illumination now; he could make out the walls, about as far apart from each other as those in a burrow, but—unlike a burrow's walls—oddly straight and at right angles to the floor and ceiling. Far off there was an immense patch of darkness. *The burrow will open out into a great big space, a real big and real dark space.*

What was this place, he wondered? What was it to the Monsters?

He had to take another look behind, into the open. One more quick look. He was going to be Eric the Eye. An Eye should be able to look at anything. He had to take another look.

But guardedly, guardedly.

Eric turned again, opening his eyes a little at a time. He clamped his teeth together so as not to cry out. Even so, he almost did. He shut his eyes quickly, waited, then opened them again.

Bit by bit, effort by effort, he found he was able to look into the great open whiteness without losing control of himself. It was upsetting, overpowering, but if he didn't look too long at any one time, he could stand it.

Distance. Enormous, elongated, unbelievable distance. Space upon space upon space—that white light bathing it all. Space far ahead, space on all sides, space going on and on until it seemed to have no end to it at all. But there, fantastically far off, there was an end. There was a wall, a wall made by giants that finally sealed off the tremendous space. It rose hugely from the flat, huge floor and disappeared somewhere far overhead.

And in between—once you could stand to look at it this much—in between, there were objects. Enormous objects, dwarfed only by the greatness of the space which surrounded them, enormous; terribly alien objects. Objects like nothing you had ever imagined.

NO, that wasn't quite true. That thing over there. Eric recognized it.

A great, squat thing like a full knapsack without the straps. Since early boyhood, many was the time he had heard it described by warriors back from an expedition into Monster territory.

There was food in that sack and the others like it. Enough food in that one sack to feed the entire population of Mankind for unnumbered auld lang synes. A different kind of food in each sack.

No spear point possessed by Mankind would cut through the fabric of its container, not near the bottom where it was thickest. Warriors had to climb about halfway up the sack, Eric knew, before they could find a place thin enough to carve themselves an entrance. Then the lumps of food would be lowered from man to man all the way down the sack, warriors clinging to precarious hand holds every few paces.

Once the pile on the floor was great enough, they would clamber down and fill their specially large, food-expedition knapsacks. Then back to the burrows and to the women who alone possessed the lore of determining whether the food was fit for consumption and of preparing it if it were.

That's where he would be at this moment, on that sack, cutting a hole in it, if he'd chosen a first category Theft like most other youths. He'd be cutting a hole, scooping out a handful of food—any quantity, no matter how small, was acceptable on an initiatory Theft—and be preparing to go home to plaudits from the women and acceptance from the men. He'd be engaged in a normal, socially acceptable endeavor.

Instead of which…

He found that he was able to stare at the Monster room now from under the cover of his hiding place with only a slight feeling of nausea. Well, that in itself was an achievement. After only a short time, here he was, able to look around and estimate the nature of Monster goods like the most experienced warrior. He couldn't look up too high as yet, but what warrior could?

Well and good, but this wasn't getting him anywhere. He didn't have a normal Theft to make. His was third category. Monster souvenirs.

Eric turned and faced the darkness again. He walked rapidly forward into the straight-walled burrow, the glow-lamp on his forehead lighting a yellow path. Ahead of him, the great black space grew steadily larger as he pushed towards it.

Everything about his Theft, his initiation into manhood, was extraordinary. Thomas the Trap-Smasher telling the women about his special talents, so that he would be accorded a vision and a name that would fit with them. Visions were supposed to come from the ancestors, through the ancestor-science of the record machine. Nobody was supposed to have the slightest idea in advance of what the vision would be. That was all up to the ancestors and their mysterious plans for their descendants.

WAS it possible, was it conceivable, that all visions and names were pre-arranged, that the record machine was set in advance for every initiation? Where did that leave religion? If that were so, how could you continue to believe in logic, in cause and effect?

And having someone—a Stranger, at that!—help you make your Theft. A Theft was supposed to be purely and simply a test of your male potential; by definition, it was something you did alone.

But if you could accept the concept of pre-arranged visions, why not pre-arranged Thefts?

Eric shook his head. He was getting into very dark corridors mentally. His world was turning into sheer and utter confusion.

But one thing he knew. Making an arrangement with a Stranger, as his uncle had done, was definitely an act contrary to all the laws and practices of Mankind. Thomas's uncertain speech had underlined that fact. It was—well, it was *wrong*.

Yet his uncle was the greatest man in all Mankind, so far as Eric was concerned. Thomas the Trap-Smasher could do no wrong. But Thomas the Trap-Smasher was evidently leaning toward Alien-science. Alien-science was wrong. But again, on the other hand, his parents, according to the Trap-Smasher, his father and his mother had been Alien-sciencers.

Too much. There was just too much to work out. There was too much he didn't know. He'd better concentrate on his Theft.

The strange burrow had come to an end. The hairs rose on the back of his neck as he walked into the great dark area and sensed enormous black heights above him. He began to hurry, turning every once in a while to make certain that he was staying in a straight line with the light from the entrance. Here, his forehead glow lamp was almost no use at all. He didn't like this place. It felt almost like being out in the open.

What, he wondered again feverishly, was this structure in the world of the Monsters? What function did it have? He was not sure he wanted to know.

Eric was running by the time he came to the end of the open space. He hit the wall so hard that he was knocked over backwards.

For a moment, he was badly frightened, then he realized what had happened. He hadn't taken his bearings for a while; he must have moved off at an angle.

Groping along the wall with extended arms, he found the entrance to the low burrow at last. It was quite low—he had to bend his knees and duck his head as he went up to. It was an unpleasantly narrow little corridor. But then there was an opening on his right—the fork his uncle had told him about—and he turned into it with relief.

He had arrived.

There was a burst of light from a group of glow lamps. And there were Strangers, there were several Strangers here. Three of them—no, four—no, five! They squatted in a corner of this large, square burrow, three of them talking earnestly, the other two engaged in some incomprehensible task with materials that were mostly unfamiliar.

ALL OF them leaped to their feet as he trotted in and deployed instantly in a wide semi-circle facing him. Eric wished desperately he had been holding two heavy spears instead of the single light one. With two heavy spears you had both a shield and a dangerous offensive weapon. A light spear was good for a single cast, and that was that.

He held it nevertheless in the throwing position above his shoulder and glared fiercely, as a warrior of Mankind should. If he had to throw, he decided, he would spring to one side immediately afterward and try to pluck the two heavy spears from his back-sling. But if they rushed him right now—

"Who are you?" asked a strong-faced, middle-aged man in the center of the semi-circle, his spear throbbing in an upraised arm. "What's your name what's your people?"

"Eric the Only," Eric told him quickly. Then he remembered to add: "I'm destined to be Eric the Eye. My people are Mankind."

"He's expected, one of us," the middle-aged man told the others who immediately relaxed, slung their spears, and went back to what they had been doing. "Welcome, Eric the Only of Mankind. Put up your spear and sit with us. I am Arthur the Organizer."

Eric gingerly dropped his spear into the back-sling. He studied the Stranger.

A man about as old as his uncle and not nearly as hefty, although well muscled enough for normal warlike purposes. He wore the loin straps of a full warrior, but—as if these were not enough honor for a man—he also wore straps laced about his chest and across his shoulders, though he was carrying no knapsack. This was the fashion of many Strangers, Eric knew, as was the strap at the back of the head that held the hair in a tight tail away from the eyes instead of letting it hang wild and free as the hair of a warrior should. And the straps were decorated with odd, incised designs—another weak and unmanlike Stranger fashion.

Who cut Strangers, Eric thought contemptuously, would group up so in an alien place without setting sentries at either end of their burrow? Truly Mankind had good reason to despise them!

But this man was a leader, he realized, a born leader, with an even more self-assured air than Thomas the Trap-Smasher, captain of the best band in all Mankind. He was studying Eric in turn, with eyes that weighed carefully and then, having decided on the measure, made a definite placement, fitting Eric permanently into this plan or that plan. He looked like a man whose head was full of many plans, each one evolving inexorably through action to a predetermined end.

He took Eric's arm companionably and led him to where the others squatted and talked and worked. This was no tribal burrow of any sort; it was quite apparently a field headquarters—and Arthur the Organizer was Commander-in-Chief. "I met your uncle," he told Eric, "about a dozen auld lang synes ago, when he came to us on a trading expedition—back in our burrows, I mean. A fine man, your uncle, very progressive. He's attended our secret meetings

THE MEN IN THE WALLS

regularly, and there's going to be an important place for him in the great burrows we will dig, in the new world we are making. He reminds me a lot of your father. But so do you, my boy, so do I you."

"Did you know my father?"

ARTHUR the Organizer smiled I and nodded. "Very well. He could have been a great man. He gave his life for the Cause. Who among us will ever forget Eric the—the— Eric the Store-keeper or something, wasn't it?"

"The Storeroom-Stormer. His name was Eric the Storeroom-Stormer."

"Yes, of course. Eric the Storeroom-Stormer. An unforgettable name with us, and an unforgettable man. But that's another story and we'll talk about it some other time. You'll have to be getting back to your uncle very soon." He picked up a flat board covered with odd markings and studied it with his glow lamp.

"How do you like that?" one of the men working with the unfamiliar materials muttered to his neighbor. "You ask him his people, and he says, 'Mankind.' *Mankind!*"

The other man chuckled. "A front-burrow tribe. What the hell do you expect—sophistication? Each and every front-burrow tribe calls itself Mankind. As far as these primitives are concerned, the human race stops at their outermost burrow. Your tribe, my tribe—you know what they call us? Strangers. In their eyes, there's not too much difference between us and the Monsters."

"That's what I mean. They don't see us as fellow men. They are narrow-minded savages. Who needs them?"

Arthur the Organizer glanced at Eric's face. He turned sharply to the man who had spoken last.

"I'll tell you who needs them, Walter," he said. "The Cause needs them. If the front-burrow tribes are with us, it means our main lines of supply to Monster territory are kept open. But we need every fighter we can get, no matter how primitive. Every single tribe has to be with us if Alien-science is to be the dominant religion of the burrows, if we're to avoid the fiasco of the last rising. We need front-burrow men for their hunting, foraging skills and back-burrow men for their civilized skills. We need everybody in this thing, especially now."

The man called Walter put down his work and scowled at Eric dubiously. He seemed to be totally unconvinced.

These arrogant back-burrowers with their ornamented straps and unmilitary manners! Men from different tribes sitting around and talking, when—if they had any sense of propriety at all—they should be killing each other!

Suddenly, the floor shook under him. He almost fell. He staggered back and forth, trying to grab at the spears in his back-sling. He finally got used to it, managed to find a solid footing in the upheaval. The spear he held vibrated in his hand.

FROM far away came a series of ear-splitting thumps. The floor swung to their rhythm. "What is it?" he cried, turning to Arthur. "What's going on?"

"You've never heard a Monster walking before?" the Organizer asked him unbelievingly. "That's right—this is your Theft, your first time out. It's a Monster, boy. A Monster's moving around in the Monster larder, doing whatever Monsters do. They have a right, you know," he added with a smile. "It's their larder. We're just—visitors."

Eric noticed that none of the others seemed particularly concerned. He drew a deep breath and reslung his spear. How the floor and the walls shook! What a fantastic, enormous creature that must be!

As an apprentice warrior, he had often stood with the rear guard on the other side of the doorway to Monster territory while the band went in to steal for Mankind. A few times then had been heavy, thumping noise off in the distance, and the wall of the burrow had quivered slightly. But not like this. It had never been remotely as awesome as this.

He raised his eyes to the straight, flat ceiling of the burrow above them. He remembers the dark space further back stretching up limitlessly. "And this," he said aloud. "This structure we're in. What is *this* to them?"

Arthur the Organizer shrugged. "A piece of Monster furniture. Something they use for something or other. We're in one of the open spaces they always leave in the bases of their furniture. Makes the furniture lighter, easier to move around, I guess." He listened for a moment as the thumps drifted further away and then died out. "Let's get down to business. Eric, this is Walter the Weapon-Seeker. Walter the Weapon-Seeker of the Miximilian people. Walter, what do you have for Eric's tribe—for, uh, for Mankind?"

"I hate to give anything even halfway good to a front-burrow tribe," the squatting man muttered. "No matter how much you explain it to them, they always use it wrong, they botch it up every single time. Let's see. This should be simple enough."

He rummaged in the pile of strange stuff in front of him and picked up a small, red, jelly-like blob. "All you do," he explained, "is tear off a pinch with your fingers. Just a pinch at a time, no more. Then spit on it and throw it. After you spit on it, get it out of your hands fast. Throw it as fast and as far as you can. Do you think you can remember that?"

"Yes." Eric took the red blob from him and stared at it in puzzlement. There was a strange, irritating odor; it made his nose itch slightly. "But what happens? What does it do?"

"That's not your worry, boy," Arthur the Organizer told him. "Your uncle will know when to use it. You have your third category theft—a Monster souvenir that no one in your tribe has ever seen before. It should make them sit up and take notice. And tell your uncle to bring his hand to my burrow three days—three sleep-periods—from now. That will be the last time we meet before the rising. Tell him to bring them armed with every last spear they can carry."

ERIC nodded weakly. There were so many complex, incomprehensible things going on! The world was a bigger, more active place than he had ever imagined.

He watched Arthur the Organizer add a mark to the flat board on which many symbols were scratched. This was another Stranger practice—made necessary, he knew, by the weak Stranger memory, so inferior to that of Mankind.

The Weapon-Seeker leaped up and stopped him as he was about to put the red blob into the knapsack. "Nothing wet in there?" Walter demanded, opening the bag and rummaging about in Eric's belongings. "No water? Remember, get this stuff wet and you're done for."

"Mankind keeps its water in canteens," Eric explained irritably. "We keep it here," he pointed to the sloshing pouch at his hip, "not splashing around loosely with our provisions." He swung the full knapsack on his back and stepped away with stiff dignity.

Arthur the Organizer accompanied him to the end of the burrow. "Don't mind Walter," he whispered. "He's always afraid that nobody but himself will be able to use the Monster weapons he digs up. He talks that way to everyone. Now, suppose I refresh your memory about the way back. We don't want you to get lost."

"I won't get lost," Eric said coldly. "I have a good memory, and I know enough to perform a simple reversal of the directions on the way here. Besides, I am Eric the Espier, Eric the Eye of Mankind. I won't get lost."

He was rather proud of himself as he trotted away, without turning his head. Let the Strangers know what you think of them. The snobs. The stuck-up bastards.

But still, he felt damaged somehow, made less—as when Roy the Runner had called him a singleton before the entire band. And the last comment he had heard behind him, "These primitives…so damned touchy," made it no better.

He crossed the dark open space, still brooding, his eyes fixed on the patch of white light ahead, his mind engaged in a completely unaccustomed examination of values. Mankind's free simplicity against the Stranger multiplicity and intricacy. Mankind's knowledge of basics, the important foraging basics of day-to-day life, against the Stranger knowledge of so many things and techniques he had never even heard about. Surely Mankind's way was infinitely preferable, far superior?

Then why did his uncle want to get mixed up with Stranger politics, he wondered, as he emerged from the structure? He turned left and, passing the small entrance he had ignored before, sped for the wall that separated him from the burrows. And why did all these Strangers, evidently each from a different tribe, agree in the contempt with which they held Mankind?

He had just turned right along the wall, on the last stretch before the doorway, when the floor shook again, jarring him out of his thoughts. He bounced up and down, frozen with fear where he stood.

He was out in the open while a Monster was abroad. A Monster had come into the larder again.

CHAPTER FIVE

FAR OFF in the dazzling distance, he caught sight of the tremendously long gray body he had heard about since childhood, higher than a hundred men standing on each other's shoulders, the thick gray legs each wider than two hefty men standing chest to chest. He caught just one wide-eyed, fear-soluble glimpse of the thing before he went into complete panic.

His panic was redeemed by a single inhibition: he didn't spring forward and run away from the wall. But that was only because it would have meant running directly toward the Monster. For one thoroughly insane moment, however, he thought of trying to claw his way through the wall against which his shoulders were pressed.

Then—because it was the direction he had been running in—he remembered the doorway. He must be about thirty, thirty-five paces from it. There lay safety: his uncle, the band, Mankind and the burrows—the blessed, closed-in, narrow burrows!

Eric leaped along the wall for the doorway. He ran as he'd never in his life run before, as he'd never imagined he could run.

But even as he fled madly, almost weeping at the effort he was making, a few sane thoughts—the result of long, tiresome drills as an initiate—organized themselves in his screaming mind. He had been closer to the structure in which the Strangers were hiding, the structure which Arthur the Organizer explained was a piece of Monster furniture. He should have turned the other way, towards the structure, gotten between it and the wall. There, unless he'd been seen as the Monster entered the larder, he could have rested safely until it was possible to make his escape.

He had gone too far to turn back now. But run silently, he reminded himself; run swiftly but make no noise, make no noise at all. According to the lessons that the warriors taught, at this distance Monster hearing was more to be feared than Monster vision. Run silently. Run for your life.

He reached the door. It had been set back in place!

In disbelief and utter horror he stared at the curved line in the wall that showed where the door had been replaced in its socket. But this was never done! This had never been heard of!

Eric beat frantically on the door with his fists. Would his knuckles make enough noise to penetrate the heavy slab? Or just enough to attract the Monster's attention?

He twisted his head quickly—a look, a deliberately wasted moment, to estimate the closeness of his danger. The Monster's legs moved so slowly; its speed would have been laughable if the very size of those legs didn't serve to push it forward an incredible distance with each step. And there was nothing laughable in that long, narrow neck, almost as long as the rest of the body, and the malevolent, relatively tiny head on the end of the neck. And those horrible pink things, all around the neck, just behind the head—

It was much nearer than it had been just seconds ago, but whether it had noticed him and was coming at him he had no idea. Beat at the door with the shaft of a spear? That should attract attention that might be heard.

Yes, by the Monster too.

THERE was only one thing to do. He stepped a few paces back from the wall. Then he leaped forward, smashing his shoulder into the door. He felt it give a little. Another try.

The floor-shaking thumps of the Monster's steps were now so close as to be almost deafening. At any moment, a great gray foot might come down and grind out his life. Eric stepped back again, forcing himself not to look up.

Another leap, another bruising collision with the door. It had definitely moved. An indentation showed all around it.

Was he about to be stepped on—to be squashed?

Eric put his hands on the door. He pushed. Slowly, suckingly, it left the place out of which it had been carved long ago.

Where was the Monster? How close? How Close?

Suddenly, the door fell over into the burrow, and Eric spilled painfully on top of it. He scrambled to his feet and darted down the corridor.

He had no time to feel relief. His mind was repeating its lessons, reminding him what he had to do next in such a situation.

Run a short distance down the burrow. Then stop and wait on the balls of your feet, ready to bolt. Get as much air into your lungs as possible. You may need it. If you hear a hissing, whistling sound, stop breathing and start running. Hold your breath for as long as you can— as long as you possibly can—then suck another chestful of air and keep running. Keep this up until you are far away. Far, far away.

Eric waited, poised to run, his back to the doorway.

Don't look around—just face the direction you'll have to run. There's only one thing you have to worry about, only one thing you have to listen for. A hissing, whistling sound. When you hear it, hold your breath and run.

He waited, his muscles contracted for instant action.

Time went by. He remembered to count. If you counted up to five hundred, slowly, and nothing happened, you were likely to be all right. You could assume the Monster probably hadn't noticed you.

So the experienced warriors said, the men who had lived through such an experience.

Five hundred. He reached five hundred and, just to be on the safe side, still tense, still ready to run, counted another five hundred, up to the ultimate number conceived by man, a full thousand.

No hissing, no whistling sounds.

No suggestion of danger.

He relaxed, and his muscles—suddenly set free—gave way. He fell to the floor of the burrow, whimpering with the release of tension.

It was over. His Theft was over. He was a man.

HE had been in the same place as a Monster, and lived through it. He had met Strangers and dealt with them as a representative of Mankind. Such things as he would have to tell his uncle!

His uncle. Where was his uncle? Where was the band?

Suddenly fully aware of how much was wrong, Eric scrambled to his feet and walked cautiously back to the open doorway. The burrow was empty. They hadn't waited for him.

But that was another incredible thing! A band never gave an initiate up for lost until at least two full days had gone by. In the chief's absence, of course, this was measured by the sleep periods of the band captain. Any band would wait two days before giving up and turning homeward. And, Eric was positive, his uncle would have waited a bit longer than that for *him*. He'd been away for such a short time! Then what had happened?

He crept to the doorway and peeped outside. There was almost no dizziness this time. His eyes adjusted quickly to the different scale of distance. The Monster was busy on the other side of the larder. It had merely been crossing the room, then, not pursuing and attacking. Apparently it hadn't noticed him at all.

Fantastic. And with all the noise he had made! All that rushing back and forth, that battering-down of the door!

The Monster turned abruptly, walked a few gigantic steps and hurled itself at the structure in which Eric had met the Strangers. The walls, the floor, everything, shook mightily in sympathy to the impact of the great organism as it wriggled a bit and became still.

Eric was startled until he realized that the creature had done no more than lie down in the structure. It was a piece of Monster furniture, after all.

How had that felt to Arthur the Organizer and Walter the Weapon-Seeker and the others hidden in the base? Eric grinned. Those Strangers must be a little less haughty, a little more sober at this moment.

Meanwhile, he had work to do, things to find out.

He got his fingers under the slab of door and tugged it upright. It was heavy! He pushed against it, slowly, carefully, first one side and then the other, walking it back to the hole in the wall. A final push, and it slid into place tightly, only the thin, curved line suggesting its existence.

Now he could look around. There had been a fight here—that much was certain. A brief, bitter battle. Examining the area closely, Eric saw unmistakable signs of conflict.

A broken spear shaft. Some blood on the wall. Part of a torn knapsack. No bodies, of course. You were not likely to find bodies after a battle. Any people of the burrows knew that the one unavoidable imperative of victory was to drag the bodies away and dispose of them. No one might ever leave dead enemies to rot where they would foul the corridors.

SO there had been a battle. He had been right—his uncle and his uncle's band had not just gone off and left him. There must have been an attack by a superior force. The band had stood its ground for a while, sustained some losses, and then been forced to retreat.

But there were a few things that didn't make sense. First, it was very unusual for a war party of Strangers to come this close to Monster territory. The burrows, which were inhabited by Mankind, the natural goal of a war party, were much further back. At this point, you would not expect to find any group larger than a foraging expedition—a Stranger band at most.

His uncle's men, fully armed, operating under battle alert, could easily cope with a single band of weavers, weaponsmiths or traders from the decadent back burrows. They would have driven them off, possibly taking a few prisoners, and continued to wait for him.

That left only two possibilities. The unlikely war party—a two or three-band attack—and, even more unlikely, a band from another fierce, front-burrow people. But front-burrowers rarely went prowling at random near Monster territory. They would have their own door cut into it and would tend to feel hugely uncertain about one belonging to another people. They too would head for the inhabited burrows if they were on any business other than the important one of stealing for their tribe's needs.

And another thing. Unless his uncle's band had been wiped out to the very last man—a thought Eric rejected as highly improbable—the survivors were honor-bound, by their oath of manhood, after doing whatever the immediate military situation required, from pursuit to retreat, to return as soon as possible to the spot where an initiate was expected back from his Theft. No warrior would dare face the women if he failed to do this.

Possibly the attack had just come. Possibly his uncle's band was a short distance away, still fighting their way from burrow's end to burrow's end; and, once they had gotten clear of the enemy, would make their way back to him.

No. In that case, he should be able to hear the battle still going on. And the burrows were dreadfully still.

Eric shivered. A warrior was not meant to be abroad without companions. He'd heard of tribeless Strangers— once, as a child, he remembered enjoying the intricate execution of a man who'd been expelled from his own people for some major crime and who had wandered pathetically into the neighborhood of Mankind—but these people were hardly to be considered human: tribes, bands, societies, were the surroundings of human creatures.

It was awful to be alone. It was unthinkable.

WITHOUT bothering to eat, though he was quite hungry after his Theft, he began walking rapidly down the corridor. After a while, he broke into a trot. He wanted to get home as soon as possible—to be among his own kind again.

He reached into his back-sling and got a spear for each hand.

A nervous business going through the corridors all by yourself. They were so empty and so quiet. They hadn't seemed this quiet when he'd been on expedition with the band. And so fearfully, frighteningly dim. Eric had never before realized how much difference there was between the light you got from one forehead glow-lamp and the usual band complement of a half-dozen. He found himself getting more and more wary of the unexpected shadows where the wall curved sharply; he picked up speed as he ran past the black hole of a branching burrow.

At anyone of those places, an enemy could be waiting for him, warned by the sound of his approaching footsteps. It could be the same enemy that had attacked his uncle's band, a handful of cruel and murderous Strangers, or a horde of them. It could be something worse. Abruptly he remembered legends of unmentionable creatures that lurked in the empty burrows, creatures who fled before the approach of a band of warriors, but who would come noiselessly upon a single man. Big creatures who engulfed you. Tiny creatures who came in their hundreds and nibbled you to pieces. Eric kept jerking his head around to look behind him; at least he could keep his doom from taking him by surprise.

It was *awful* to be alone.

And yet, in the midst of his fears, his mind returned again and again to the problem of his uncle's disappearance. Eric could not believe anything serious had happened to him. Thomas the Trap-Smasher was a veteran of too many bloody adventures, too many battles against unequal odds. Then where had he gone? And where had he taken the band?

And why was there no sound of him anywhere, no sign in all this infinity of gloomy, stretching, menace-filled tunnels?

Fortunately, he was an Eye. He knew the way back and sped desperately along it without the slightest feeling of doubt. The Record Machine was right—he would never be lost. Let him just get safely back to the companionship of Mankind and he would be Eric the Eye.

And there it was again: who had been right, the Record Machine or his uncle? The vision that named him had come from the Record Machine, but his uncle claimed that this was religious claptrap. The vision had been selected and his name proposed to the women well in advance of the ceremony. And his uncle was an Alien-sciencer, in touch with Strangers who were also Alien-sciencers...

So many things had happened in the last two days, Eric felt. So much of his world had shifted. It was as if the walls of the burrows had moved outward and upward until they resembled Monster territory more than human areas.

HE WAS getting close now. These corridors looked friendlier, more familiar. He made himself run faster, although he was almost at the point of exhaustion. He wanted to be home, to be officially Eric the Eye, to inform Mankind of what had happened so that a rescue and searching party could be sent out for his uncle.

That doorway to Monster territory—who had replaced it? If a battle had been fought, and his uncle's band had retreated, still fighting, would the attacker have stopped to put the door neatly back in its socket? No.

Could it be explained by a sudden onslaught and the complete extermination of his uncle's band? Then, before dragging the bodies away, the enemy would have had time to put the door back. A doorway into Monster territory was a valuable human resource, after all, valuable to Mankind and Strangers alike—why jeopardize it by leaving it visible and open?

But who—or what—could have been capable of such a sudden onslaught, such a complete extermination of the best-led band in all Mankind? He'd have to get the answer from one of the other band captains or possibly a wise old crone in the Female Society.

Definitely within the boundaries of Mankind now, Eric forced himself to slow to a walk. He would be coming upon a sentry at any moment, and he had no desire at all to have a spear flung through him. A sentry would react violently to a man dashing out of the darkness.

"Eric the Only," he called out, identifying himself with each step. "This is Eric the Only." Then he remembered his Theft proudly and changed the identification. "Eric the Eye.

This is Eric the Eye, the Espier, the further-seeing, less-paying Eye. Eric the Eye is coming back to Mankind!"

Oddly, there was no returning call of recognition. Eric didn't understand that. Had Mankind itself been attacked and driven away from its burrow? A sentry should respond to a familiar name. Something was very, inexplicably wrong.

Then he came around the last curve and saw the sentry at the other end. Rather, he saw what at first looked like three sentries. They were staring at him, and he recognized them. Stephen the Strong-Armed and two members of Stephen's band. Evidently he had arrived just at the moment when the sentry on duty was about to be relieved. That would account for Stephen and the other man. But why hadn't they replied to his shouts of identification?

They stood there silently as he came up, their spears still at the ready, not going down in welcome. "Eric the Eye," he repeated, puzzled. "I've made my Theft, but something happened to the rest—"

His voice trailed off, as Stephen came up to him, his face grim, his powerful muscles taut. The band captain shoved a spear point hard against Eric's chest. "Don't move," he warned. "Barney. John. Tie him up. We've caught the little rat!"

CHAPTER SIX

HIS spears taken from him, his arms bound securely behind his back by the thongs of his own knapsack, Eric was pushed and prodded into the great central burrow of Mankind.

The place was almost unrecognizable.

Under the direction of Ottilie, the Chieftain's First Wife, a horde of women—what seemed at first like the entire membership of the Female Society—was setting up a platform in front of the Royal Mound. With the great scarcity of any building materials that Mankind suffered from, a construction of this sort was startling and unusual, yet there was something about it that awoke highly unpleasant memories in Eric's mind. But he was pulled from place to place too fast and there were too many other unprecedented things going on for him to be able to identify the memory properly.

Two women who were accredited members of the Female Society were not working under Ottilie's direction, he noticed. Bound hand and foot, they were lying against the far wall of the great central burrow. They were both covered with blood and showed every sign of having undergone prolonged and most vicious torture. He judged them to be barely this side of death.

As he was jerked past, he recognized them. They were the two wives of Thomas the Trap-Smasher.

Just wait until his uncle got back! Someone would really pay for this, he thought, more in absolute amazement than horror. He had the feeling that he must keep the horror away at all costs. Once let it in and it would soak through his thoughts right into the memory he was trying to avoid.

The place was full of armed men, running back and forth from their band captains to unknown destinations in the outlying corridors. Between them and around them scuttled the children, fetching and carrying raw materials for the hard-working women. There was a steady buzz of commands in the air…"Go to—" "Bring some more—" "Hurry with the—"…that mingled with the smell of many people whose pores were sweating urgency. And it wasn't just sweat that he smelled. Eric realized as he was dragged before the Royal Mound. It was anger. The anger and fear of all Mankind.

Franklin the Father of Many Thieves stood on the mound carrying unaccustomed spears in his fat hands, talking rapidly to a group of warriors, band captains and—yes, actually!—*Strangers*. Even now, Eric found he could still be astonished at this fantastic development.

Strangers in the very midst of Mankind! Walking around freely and bearing arms!

As the chief caught sight of Eric, his face broke into a loose-skinned smile. He nudged a Stranger beside him and pointed at the prisoner.

"That's him," he said. "That's the nephew. The one that asked for the third category Theft. Now we've got them all."

The Stranger didn't smile. He looked briefly at Eric and turned away. "I'm glad you think so. From our point of view, you've just got one more."

FRANKLIN'S smile faded to an uncertain grin. "Well, you know what I mean. And the damned fool came back by himself. It saved us a lot of trouble, I mean, didn't it?" Receiving no answer, he shrugged. He gestured with flabby imperiousness at Eric's guards. "You know where to put him. We'll be ready for them pretty soon."

Again the point of a spear stabbed into Eric's back, and he was forced forward across the central space to a small burrow entrance. Before he could reach it, however, he heard Franklin the Father of Many Thieves call out to Mankind: "There goes Eric, my people. Eric the Only. Now we've got the last of the filthy gang!"

For a moment, the activity stopped and seemed to focus on him. Eric shivered as a low drawn-out grunt of viciousness and hatred arose everywhere, but most of all from the women. Someone ran up to him. Harriet the History-Teller. The girl's face was absolutely contorted. She reached up to the crown of her head and pulled out the long pin held in place by a few knotted scarlet hairs. About her face and neck the hair danced like flames.

"You Alien-sciencer!" she shrieked, driving the pin straight at his eyes. "You filthy, filthy Alien-sciencer!"

Eric whipped his head to one side; she was back at him in a moment. His guards leaped at the girl and grappled with her, but she was able to get in one ripping slash that opened up almost all of his right cheek before they drove her away.

"Leave something for the rest of us," one of his guards pleaded the cause of reason as he strolled back to Eric. "After all, he belongs to the whole of Mankind."

"He does not!" she yelled. "He belongs to me most of all. I was going to mate with him when he returned from his Theft, wasn't I Mother?"

"There wasn't anything official," Eric heard Rita the Record-keeper admonishing as he tried to stanch the flow of blood by bringing his shoulder up and pressing it against the wound. "There couldn't be anything official about it until he'd achieved manhood. So you'll just have to wait your turn, Harriet, darling. You'll have to wait until your elders are finished with him. There'll be plenty left for you."

"There won't be," the girl pouted. "I know what you're like. There won't be hardly anything left."

Eric was shoved at the small burrow entrance again. The moment he was inside it, one of his guards planted a boot in his back, knocking the breath out of him. The kick propelled him forward, staggering wildly for balance, until he smashed into the opposite wall. As he fell, unable to use his arms to cushion himself, he heard laughter behind him in the great central burrow. He rolled on his side dizzily. There was a fresh flow of blood coming down from his cheek.

This wasn't the homecoming he'd imagined after his Theft—not in the slightest! What was going on?

He knew where he was. A tiny, blind-alley burrow off Mankind's major meeting-place, a sort of little vault used mostly for storage. Excess food and goods stolen from Monster territory were kept here until there was enough accumulated for a trading expedition to the back burrows. Occasionally, also, a male Stranger, taken prisoner in battle, might be held in this place until Mankind found out if his tribe valued him enough to pay anything substantial for his recovery.

And if they didn't...

ERIC remembered the unusual structure that the women had been building near the Royal Mound—and shivered. The memory that he'd suppressed had now come alive in his mind. And it fitted with the way Harriet had acted—and with what her mother, Rita the Record-Keeper, had said.

They couldn't be planning that for him! He was a member of Mankind, almost a full warrior. They didn't even do that to Strangers captured in battle—not *normal* Strangers. A warrior was always respected as a warrior. At the worst, he deserved a decent execution, quietly done. Except for— Except for—

"No!" he screamed. *"No!"*

The single guard who'd been left on duty at the entrance turned around and regarded him humorously.

"Oh, yes," he said. "Oh, definitely yes! We're going to have a lot of fun with both of you, as soon as the women say they're ready." He nodded with ominous, emphatic slowness and turned back to miss none of the preparations.

Both of you? For the first time, Eric looked around the little storage burrow. The place was almost empty of goods, but off to one side, in the light of his forehead glow-lamp (how proud he had been when it had been bestowed on him at the doorway to Monster territory!) he now saw another man lying bound against the wall.

His uncle.

Eric brought his knees up and wriggled rapidly over to him. It was a painful business. His belly and sides were not callused and inured to the rough burrow floor like his feet. But what did a few scratches more or less matter any more?

The Trap-Smasher was barely conscious. He had been severely handled, and he looked almost as bad as his wives. There was a thick crust of dried blood on his hair. The shaft of a spear, Eric guessed, had all but cracked his head open. And in several places on his body, his right shoulder, just above his left hip, deep in his thigh, were the oozing craters of serious spear wounds, raw and unbandaged.

"Uncle Thomas," Eric urged. "What happened? Who did this to you?"

THE wounded man opened his eyes and shuddered. He looked around stupidly as if he had expected to find the walls talking to him. And his powerful arms struggled with the knots that held them firmly behind his back. When he finally located Eric, he smiled.

It was a bad thing to do. Someone had also smashed in most of his front teeth.

"Hello, Eric," he mumbled, "what a fight, eh? How did the rest of the band do? Anybody get away?"

"I don't know. That's what I'm asking *you!* I came back from my Theft—you were gone—the band was gone. I got here, and everyone's crazy! There are Strangers out there, walking around with weapons in our burrows. Who are they?"

Thomas the Trap-Smasher', eyes had slowly darkened. They were fully in focus now, and long threads of agony swam in them. "Strangers?" he asked in a low voice. "Yes, there were Strangers fighting in Stephen the Strong-Armed's band. Fighting against us. That chief of ours—Franklin—he got in touch with Strangers after we left. They compared notes. They must have been working together, been in touch with each other, for a long time. Mankind, Strangers, what difference does it make when their lousy Ancestor-science is threatened? I should have remembered."

"What?" Eric begged. "What should you have remembered?"

"That's the way they put down Alien-science in the other rising, long ago. A chief's a chief. He's got more in common with another chief—even a chief of Strangers—than with his own people. You attack Ancestor-Science, and you're attacking their power as chiefs. They'll work together then. They'll give each other men, weapons, information. They'll do everything they can against the common enemy. Against the only people who really want to hit back at the Monsters. I should have remembered! Damn it all," the Trap-Smasher groaned through his ruined mouth, "I saw that the chief and Ottilie were suspicious. I should have realized how they were going to handle it. They were going to call in Strangers, exchange information—and unite against us!"

Eric stared at his uncle, dimly understanding. Just as there was a secret organization of Alien-sciencers that cut across tribal boundaries, so there was a tacit, rarely used understanding among the chiefs, based on the Ancestor-Science religion that was the main prop of their power. *And* the power of the leaders of the Female Society, come to think of it. All special privileges were derived from their knowledge of Ancestor-Science. Take that away from them, and they'd be ordinary women with no more magical abilities than was necessary to tell edible food from Monster poison.

Grunting with pain, Thomas the Trap-Smasher wormed his way up to a sitting position against the wall. He kept shaking his head as if to jar recollection loose.

"They came up to us," he said heavily, "Stephen the Strong-Armed and his band came up to us just after you'd gone into Monster territory. A band from Mankind with a message from the chief—who suspected anything? They might be coming to tell us that the home burrows were under attack by Strangers. Strangers!" He gave a barking laugh, and some blood splashed out of his mouth. "They had Strangers with them, hidden all the way behind in the corridors. Mobs and mobs of Strangers."

ERIC began to visualize what had happened.

"Then, when they were among us, when most of us had reslung our spears, they hit us. Eric, they hit us real good. They had us so much by surprise that they didn't even need outside help. I don't think there was much left of us by the time the Strangers came running up. I was down, fighting with my bare hands, and so was the rest of the band. The Strangers did the mopping up. I didn't see most of it. Somebody handed me one hell of a wallop—I never expected to wake up alive." His voice got even lower and huskier. "I'd have been lucky not to."

The Trap-Smasher's chest heaved; a strange, long noise came out of it. "They brought me back here. My wives— they were working on my wives. Those bitches from the Female Society—Ottilie, Rita—this part of it is their business—they had my wives pegged out and they worked on them in front of me. I was blanking out and coming to, blanking out and coming to; I was conscious while they—"

He dropped to a bloody mumble again, his head falling forward loosely. His voice became clear for a moment, but not entirely rational. "They were good women," he muttered. "Both of them. Good, good girls. And they loved me. They had their chance to become more important. A dozen times Franklin must have offered to impregnate them, and they turned him down every time. They really loved me."

Eric almost sobbed himself. He'd had little to do with them once he'd reached the age of the warrior-initiate, but in his childhood, they'd given him all the mother love he ever remembered! They'd cuffed him and caressed him and wiped his nose. They'd told him stories and taught him the catechism of the ancestral science. Neither had sons of his age who had survived the various plagues and the Monster-inflicted calamities that periodically swept through Mankind's burrows. He'd been lucky. He'd received much of the care and affection that their own sons might have enjoyed.

Their fidelity to the Trap-Smasher had been a constant source of astonishment in Mankind. It had cost them more than the large, healthy litters for which the chief had a well-proven capacity—such eccentric, almost non-womanly behavior had inevitably denied them the high positions in the Female Society they would otherwise have enjoyed.

And now they were dead or dying, and their surviving babies had been apportioned to other women whose importance would thereby be substantially increased.

"Tell me," he asked his uncle, "Why did the Female Society kill them? What did they do that was so awful?"

He saw that Thomas had lifted his head again and was staring at him, with pity. He felt his own body turn completely cold even before the Trap-Smasher spoke.

"You still won't let yourself think about it? I don't blame you, Eric. But it's there. It's being prepared for us outside."

"What?" Eric demanded, although a distant part of him had already worked out the terrible answer and knew what it was.

"We've been declared outlaws, Eric. They say we're guilty of the ultimate sacrilege against Ancestor-Science. We don't belong to Mankind anymore—you, me, my family, my band. We're outside Mankind, outside the law, outside religion. And you know what happens to outlaws, Eric, don't you? Anything goes. *Anything.*"

CHAPTER SEVEN

EVER since early childhood, Eric remembered looking forward to ceremonies of this sort. A Stranger would have been caught by one of the warrior bands, and it would he determined that he was an outlaw. Nine times out of ten, such a man was easy enough to identify. No one but an outlaw, for example, would be wandering the burrows by himself, without a band or at least a single companion to guard his back. The tenth time, when there was the slightest doubt, a request for ransom to his people would make the prisoner's position clear. There would be a story of some unforgivable sacrilege, some particularly monstrous crime that could be punished by nothing but complete anathema and the revocation of all privileges as a human being. The man had escaped the punishment being prepared for him. Do with him as you will, his people would say. He is no longer one of us; he is the same as a Monster; he is something non-human so far as we are concerned.

Then a sort of holiday would be declared. Out of the bits and pieces of lumber stolen from Monster territory and set aside by the women for this purpose, the members of the Female Society would erect a structure whose specifications had been handed down from mother to daughter for countless generations—all the way back to the ancestors who had built the Record-Machines. It was called a Stage or a Theater, although Eric had also heard it referred to as The Scaffold. In any case, whatever its true name, most of the details concerning it were part of the secret lore of the Female Society and, as such, were no proper concern of males.

One thing about it, however, everyone knew—on it would be enacted a moving religious drama: the ultimate triumph of humanity over the wickedness of the Monsters.

For this, the central character had to fulfill two requirements. He had to be an intelligent creature, as the Monsters were, so that he could be made to suffer as some day Mankind meant the Monsters to suffer; and he had to be non-human, as the Monsters were, so that every drop of fear, resentment and hatred distilled by the enormous swaggering aliens could be poured out upon his flesh without any inhibition of compunction or fellow-feeling.

For this purpose, outlaws were absolutely ideal, since all agreed that such disgusting creatures had resigned their membership in the human race.

WHEN an outlaw was caught, work stopped in the burrows, and Mankind's warrior bands were called home. It was a great time, a joyous time, a time of festival. Even the children—doing whatever they could to prepare for the glorious event, running errands for the laboring women, fetching refreshment for the stalwart, guarding men—even the children boasted to each other of how they would express their hatred upon this trapped representative of the non-human, this bound and shrieking protagonist of the utterly alien.

Everyone had their chance. All, from the chief himself to the youngest child capable of reciting the catechism of ancestral science, all climbed in their turn upon the Stage—or Theater—or Scaffold—that the women had erected. All were thrilled to vent a portion of Mankind's vengeance upon the creature who had been declared alien, as an earnest of what they would some day do collectively to the Monsters who had stolen their world.

Sarah the Sickness-Healer had her turn early in the proceedings; thenceforth, she stood on the structure and carefully supervised the ceremony. It was her job to see that nobody went too far, that everyone had a fair and adequate turn, and that even at the end there was some life left in the victim. Because then, at the end, the structure had to be completely burned—along with its bloody occupant—as a Symbol of how the Monsters must eventually be turned into ash and be blown away and vanish.

"And Mankind will come into its own," she would chant, while the charred fragments were kicked out of the burrow contemptuously. "And the Monsters will be gone. They will be gone forever, and there will be nothing upon all the wide Earth but Mankind."

Afterwards, there was feasting, there was dancing, there was singing. Men and women chased each other into the dimmer side corridors; children whooped and yelled around the great central burrow; the few old folks went to sleep with broad, reminiscent smiles upon their faces. Everyone felt they had somehow struck back at the Monsters. Everyone felt a little like the lords of creation their ancestors had been.

Eric remembered the things he himself had done—the things he had seen others do—on these occasions. A tremendous tic of fear rippled through his body. He had to draw his shoulders up to his neck in a tight hunch and tense the muscles of his arms and legs. Finally his nerves subsided.

He could think again, only he didn't want to think.

Those others, those outlaws in previous ceremonies of this sort in auld lang synes long; past—was it possible that they had experienced the same sick, bewildered dread while waiting for the structure to be completed? Had they trembled like this, had they also felt wetness running down their backs, had they felt the same pleading squirm in their intestines, the same anticipatory twinges of soft, vulnerable flesh?

THE thought had never crossed his mind before. He'd seen them as things completely outside humanity, the compressed symbol of all that was alien. One worried about their feelings no more than about those of the roaches scurrying madly about here in the storage burrow. One squashed them slowly or rapidly—at one's pleasure. What difference did it make? You didn't sympathize with roaches. You didn't identify with them.

But now that he was about to be squashed himself, he realized that it did make a difference. He was human. No matter what Mankind and its leaders now declared him to be, he was human. He felt human fears; he experienced a desperate human desire to live.

Then so had the others been. The outlaws whom he'd helped tear to pieces. Human. Completely human.

They'd sat here, just as he did now, they'd sat and waited for the festival and its agonies...

Only twice in his memory had members of Mankind ever been declared outlaw. Both cases had occurred a long time ago, before he'd even been a warrior-initiate. Eric tried now to remember what they had been like as living people. He wanted to reach out and feel companionship, some sort of companionship, even that of the dead. The dead were better than this beaten, bloody man next to him who had subsided into half-insane mumbles, his battered head on his torn and wound-scribbled chest.

What had they been like? It was no use. In the first case, memory brought back only a picture of a screaming hulk just before the fire was lit. No recollection of a man. No fellow-human in Mankind. And in the second case—

Eric sat bolt upright, straining against his bonds. The second man to be declared an outlaw had escaped! How he had done it Eric had never found out. He remembered only that a guard was severely punished, and that bands of warriors had sniffed for him along far-distant corridors for a long time afterward.

Escape. That was it. He had to escape. Once declared an outlaw, he could have no hope of mercy, no remission of sentence. The religious overtones of the ceremony being prepared were too highly charged to be halted for anything short of the disappearance of its chief protagonist.

Yes, escape. But how? Even if he could get free of the knots which so expertly and so strongly tied his hands behind his back, he had no weapon to hand. The guard at the entrance would transfix him with a spear in a moment. And if he failed, there were others outside, almost the entire warrior strength of the people.

How? *How?* He forced himself to be calm, to go over every possible alternative in his mind. He knew there was not much time. In a little while, the structure would be finished and the leaders' of the Female Society would come for him.

ERIC began working on the knots behind him. He worked without much hope. If he could get his hands loose, perhaps he might squirm his way carefully to the entrance, leap up suddenly and break into a run. So what if they threw a spear through him—wouldn't that be better and quicker than the other thing?

But they wouldn't, he realized. Not unless he were very lucky and some warrior forgot to think straight. In cases like this, when it was a matter of keeping, not killing a prisoner, you aimed for the legs. There were at least a dozen men in Mankind with skill great enough to bring him down even at twenty or twenty-five paces. And another dozen who might be able to catch him. He was no Roy the Runner, after all.

Roy! He was dead and sewered by now. He found himself regretting the fight he'd had with Roy.

A Stranger passed by the storage burrow entrance, glancing in with only a slight curiosity. He was followed in a moment by two more Strangers, going the same way. They were leaving, Eric guessed, before the ceremony began. They probably had ceremonies of their own to attend—with their own people.

Walter the Weapon-Seeker, Arthur the Organizer—were they at this moment sitting in similar storage burrows awaiting the same slow death? Eric doubted it. Somehow he couldn't see these men caught as easily as he and his uncle had been. Arthur was too clever, he was certain of that, and Walter, well, Walter would come up with some fantastic weapon that no one had ever seen or heard of...

Like the one he had in his knapsack right now—that red blob the Weapon-Seeker had given him!

Was it a weapon? He didn't know. But even if it wasn't, he had the impression it could create some kind of surprise. "It should make them sit up and take notice," Walter had said back in Monster territory.

Any kind of surprise, any kind of upset and he might have a diversion under cover of which he and his uncle could escape.

But that was the trouble. His uncle. With his hands bound as thoroughly as he could now ascertain they were, he needed his uncle's help to do anything at all. And the Trap-Smasher was obviously too far gone to be at all useful.

He was talking to himself in a steady, monotonous, argumentative mutter, his upper body slumping further and further across his own lap. Every once in a while, the mutters would be broken by a sharp, almost surprised moan as his wounds woke into a clearer consciousness of themselves.

Most other men in his condition, Eric judged, would have been dead by now. Only a body as powerful as the Trap-Smasher's could have lasted this long. And—who knew?—if they could escape, it was possible that his uncle's wounds, given care and rest, might heal.

If they could escape.

"UNCLE THOMAS," he said, leaning toward him and whispering urgently. "I think I know a way out. I think I've figured out a way to escape."

No response. The bloody head continued to talk in a low, toneless voice to the lap. Mutter, mutter, mutter. Moan. Mutter, mutter.

"Your wives," Eric said desperately. "Your wives. Don't you want to get revenge for your wives?"

That seemed to be worth a flicker. "My wives," said the thick voice. "They were good women. Real good women. They never let Franklin near them. They were real good women." Then the flicker was over and the mutters returned.

"Escape!" Eric whispered. "Don't you want to escape?"

A thin, coagulating line of blood dripped out of his uncle's slowly working jaws. There was no other answer.

Eric looked towards the entrance of the storage burrow. The guard posted there was no longer turning from time to time to glance at the prisoners. The structure outside was evidently nearing completion, and his interest in the final preparations had caused him to take a step or two away from the entrance. He was staring off to the left down the great central burrow in absolute fascination.

Well, that was something. It gave them a chance. On the other hand, it also meant that they had scant moments left to their lives. Any time now, the leaders of the Female Society would be coming to drag them to the torture ceremony.

With his eyes on the guard, Eric leaned against the rough burrow wall and began scraping the imprisoning knapsack thongs against the sharpest edges he could find. It wouldn't be fast enough, he realized. If there were only a spear point in this place, something sharp. He looked around feverishly. No, nothing. A few tumbled bags of food over which lazy roaches wandered. Nothing he could use to help him get free.

His uncle was his only hope. Somehow he had to rouse the man, get through to him. He squirmed up close, his mouth against the Trap-Smasher's battered ear.

"This is Eric, Eric the Only. Do you remember me, Uncle? I went on the Theft, Uncle Thomas, I went on the Theft with you. Third category. Remember, I asked for a third category theft, just like you told me to? I did my Theft, I was successful, I made it. I did just what you told me to do. I'm Eric the Eye now, right? Tell me, am I Eric the Eye?"

Mutters, mumbles and moans. The man seemed beyond intelligibility.

"What about Franklin? He can't do this to us, can he, Uncle Thomas? Don't you want to escape? Don't you want revenge on Franklin, on Ottilie, for what they did to your wives? Don't you? *Don't you?*"

He had to cut through his uncle's confused mist of gathering delirium.

In complete desperation, he lowered his head and sank his teeth into a wounded shoulder.

NOTHING. Just the steady flow of argumentative gibberish. And the thin blood dripping from the mouth.

"I saw Arthur the Organizer. He said he'd known you for a long time. When did you meet him, Uncle Thomas? When did you first meet Arthur the Organizer?"

The head drooped lower, the shoulders slumped further forward.

"Tell me about Alien-science. What is Alien-science?" Eric was almost gibbering himself now in his frantic efforts to find a key that would unlock his uncle's mind. "Are Arthur the Organizer and Walter the Weapon-Seeker very important men among the Alien-sciencers? Are they the chiefs? What was the name of the structure they were hiding in? What is it to the Monsters? They talked about other tribes, tribes I never heard of. How many other tribes are there? Are these other tribes?"

That was it. He had found the key. He had gotten through.

Thomas the Trap-Smasher's head came up waveringly, dimness swirling in his eyes. "Other tribes. Funny that you should ask about other tribes. That you should ask."

"Why? What about them?" Eric fought to hold the key in place, to keep it turning. "Why shouldn't I ask about those other tribes?"

"Your grandmother was from another tribe, a real strange tribe in a far-off burrow. I remember hearing about it when I was a little boy." Thomas the Trap-Smasher nodded to himself. "Your grandfather's band went on a long journey, the longest they'd ever taken. And they caught your grandmother and brought her back."

"My grandmother?" For the moment, Eric forgot what was being prepared for him outside. He'd known there was some peculiar secret about his grandmother. She had rarely been mentioned in Mankind. Up to now, he'd taken it for granted that this was because she'd had a son who was terribly unlucky—almost the worst thing a person in the burrows could be. A one-child litter, after all, and being killed together with his wife in Monster territory. Very unlucky.

"MY grandmother was from another tribe? Not from Mankind?" He knew, of course, that several of the women had been captured from other peoples in neighboring burrows and had the good fortune now to be considered full-fledged members of Mankind. Sometimes one of their own women would be lost this way, when she strayed too far down an outlying burrow and stumbled into a band of Stranger warriors. If you stole a woman from another people, after all, you stole a substantial portion of their knowledge. But he'd never imagined—

"Dora the Dream-Singer."

Thomas's head waggled loosely; he dribbled words mixed with red saliva. "Did you know why your grandmother was called the Dream-Singer, Eric? The women used to say that the things she talked about happened only in dreams, and that she couldn't talk straight like other people—she could only sing about her dreams. But she taught your father a lot, and he was like her. Women were a little afraid to mate with him. My sister was the first to take a chance—and everyone said she deserved what she got."

Abruptly, Eric became conscious of a change in the sounds outside the burrow. More quiet. Were they coming for him now?

"Uncle Thomas, listen! I have an idea. Those Strangers— Walter, Arthur the Organizer—they gave me a Monster souvenir. I don't know what it does, but I can't get at it. I'll turn around. You try to reach down into my knapsack with the tips of your fingers and—"

The Trap-Smasher paid no attention to him. "She was an Alien-sciencer," he rambled on, mostly to himself. "Your grandmother was the first Alien-sciencer we ever had in Mankind, I guess her tribe was all Alien-sciencers. Imagine— a whole tribe of Alien-sciencers!"

Eric groaned. This half-alive, delirious man was his only hope of escaping. This bloody wreck who had once been the proudest, most alert band captain of them all. I

He turned for another look at the guard. The man was still staring down the length of the great central burrow. There was nothing to be heard now but a terrifying silence, as if dozens of pairs of eyes were glowing in anticipation. And footsteps—were not those footsteps? He had to find a way to make his uncle cooperate.

"THOMAS the Trap-Smasher!" he said sharply, barely managing to keep his voice low, "Listen to me. This is an order! There's something in my knapsack, a blob of sticky stuff. We're going to turn our backs to each other, and you're going to reach in with your fingers and fish it out. Do you hear me? That's an order—a warrior's order!"

His uncle nodded, completely docile. "I've been a warrior for over twenty auld lang synes," he mumbled, twisting around. "Six of them a band captain. I've given orders and taken them, given them and taken them. I've never disobeyed an order. What I always say is how can you expect to give orders if you don't—"

"Now," Eric told him, bringing their backs together and hunching down so that his knapsack would be just under his uncle's bound arms. "Reach in. Work that mass of sticky stuff out. It's right on top. And hurry!"

Yes. Those were footsteps coming up outside. Several of them. The leaders of the Female Society, the chief, an escort of warriors. And the guard, watching that deadly procession, was liable to remember his duties and turn back to the prisoners.

"Hurry," he demanded. "I told you to hurry, dammit! That's an order, too. Get it out fast. Fast!"

And, all this time, as the Trap-Smasher's fumbling fingers wandered about in his knapsack, as he listened with fright and impatience to the sounds of the approaching execution party—all this time, somewhere in his mind, there was wonderment at the orders he was rapping out to an experienced band captain and the incredible authority he had managed to get into his voice.

"Now you're wondering where your grandmother's tribe have their burrow," Thomas began suddenly, reverting to an earlier topic as if they were having a pleasant conversation after a fine, full meal.

"Forget it! Get that stuff out. Just get it out!"

"It's hard to describe," the other man's voice wandered on. "A long way off, their burrow is, a long way off. You know the Strangers call us front-burrow people. You know that, don't you? The Strangers are back-burrowers. Well, your grandmother's people are the bottommost burrowers of all."

Eric sensed his fingers closing in the knapsack.

The three women who ruled the Female Society came into the storage burrow. Ottilie the Omen-Teller, Sarah the Sickness-Healer and Rita the Record-Keeper. With them was the chief and two band captains, heavily armed.

CHAPTER EIGHT

OTTILIE, the Chieftain's First Wife, was in the lead. She stopped, just inside the entrance to the burrow and the others came to a halt around her.

"Look at them," she jeered. "They're trying to free each other! And what do they plan to do if they get themselves untied?"

Franklin moved to her side and took a long, judicious look at the two men squatting back to back. "They'll try to escape," he explained, continuing his wife's joke. "They'll have their hands free, they figure, and surely Thomas the Trap-Smasher and his nephew are a match, even bare-handed, for the best spearmen in Mankind!"

And then Eric felt the searching hands come up out of the knapsack to which his own arms were tied. Something fell to the floor of the burrow. It made an odd noise, halfway between a splash and a thud. He twisted around for it immediately with his mouth open, flexing his knees in a tight crouch underneath his body.

"You've never seen anything like the burrows of your grandmother's people," his uncle was mumbling, as if what his hands had just done was no concern of the rest of him. "And neither have I, though I've listened to the tales."

"He won't last long now," Sarah the Sickness-Healer commented. "We'll have to have our fun with the boy."

All you do, Walter the Weapon-Seeker had said, *is tear off a pinch with your fingers. Then spit on it and throw it. Throw it as fast and as far as you can.*

He couldn't use his fingers. But he leaned down to the red blob and nipped off a piece with his teeth. He brought his tongue against the strange soft substance, lashing saliva into it. And simultaneously he kicked at the burrow floor with curved toes, straightening his legs, jerking his thighs and body upward. Unable to use his arms for balance, he tottered erect and turned, swaying, to face the leaders of his people.

After you spit on it, throw it fast. As fast and as far as you can.

"I don't know what he's doing," someone said, "but I don't like it. Let me through."

Stephen the Strong-Armed stepped ahead of the group and lifted a heavy spear, ready for throwing.

Eric shut his eyes, bent his head far back on his neck and took a deep, deep breath. Then he snapped his head forward, flipping his tongue hard against the object in his mouth. He forced out his breath so abruptly that the exhalation became a wild, barking cough.

The soft little mass flew out of his mouth, and he opened his eyes to watch its course. For a moment, he was unable to find it anywhere; then he located it by the odd expression on Stephen's face and the fearful upward roll of his eyes.

There was a little red splotch in the middle of the band captain's forehead.

What was supposed to happen, he wondered? He had followed directions as well as he could under the circumstances, but he had no idea what the scarlet stain, made loose and moist by his saliva, was supposed to accomplish. He watched it, hoping and waiting.

Then Stephen the Strong-Armed brought his free hand up slowly to wipe the stuff off. Eric stopped hoping. Nothing was going to happen

Strangers, he had begun to think despairingly, *that's what comes of trusting Strangers—*

THE blast of sound was so tremendous that for a moment he thought the roof of the burrow had fallen in. He was slammed backwards against the wall and fell as if he'd been walloped with a spear haft. He remembered the cough with which he'd expelled the bit of red blob from his mouth. Had there been a delayed echo to his cough, a gigantic, ear-splitting echo?

He lifted his head from the floor finally, when the reverberations in the little storage burrow had rumbled into a comparative silence. Someone was screaming. Someone was screaming over and over again.

It was Sarah. She was looking at Stephen the Strong-Armed from the rear. She had been standing directly behind him. Now she was staring at him and screaming in sharp steady bursts.

Her mouth was open so wide that it seemed she was about to tear her jaws apart. And with each scream she lifted her arm rigidly and pointed to the back of Stephen's neck. She kept lifting her arm and pointing as if she wanted everyone present to know beyond the least doubt why and how she came to be screaming.

Stephen the Strong-Armed had no head. His body ended at the neck, and flaps of skin fell down to his chest in an irregular wavy pattern. A fountain of blood bubbled and spurted where his head had been. His body still stood upright, feet planted wide apart in a good warrior's stance, one arm holding the spear ready for action and the other congealed in its upward motion to wipe the red blob away. It stood, incredibly straight and tall and alive.

Suddenly, it fell apart.

First the spear slid slowly forward out of the right hand and clattered to the floor. Then the arms began to fall loosely to the sagging knees and the entire great, brawny body slumped as if its bones had left it. It dropped aimlessly to the floor, an arm poking out here, a leg twisting out there, in a pattern as meaningless as if an oddly shaped bag of skin had been flung to one side of the burrow.

It continued to twitch for a moment or two, as the bubbling fountain of blood turned into a sluggishly flowing river. At last it lay still, a motionless heap of limbs and torso. Of the missing head there was no trace anywhere.

SARAH the Sickness-Healer stopped screaming and turned, shaking, to her companions. Their protruding eyes left the body on the floor.

Then they all reacted at once.

They yelled madly, wildly, fearfully, as if they were a chorus and she the conductor. Still bellowing, they made for the narrow entrance behind them. They got through in a pushing, punching scramble that at one point looked like a composite monster with dozens of arms, legs and swinging, naked breasts. They carried the guard outside with them, and with them, too, they carried their uncontrollable panic, screaming it into existence all along the great central burrow.

For a little while, Eric could hear feet pounding into the distant corridors. Then there was quiet. There was quiet everywhere, except for Thomas the Trap-Smasher's interminable mumbling.

Eric forced himself upright again. He was unable to imagine what had happened. That red blob—the Stranger, Walter, had said it was a weapon, but it didn't operate like any weapon he had ever in his life heard of. Except possibly in the times of the ancestors; the ancestors were supposed to have had things that could blow an object apart and leave no trace. But this was an alien artifact, a possession of the Monsters, which Walter the Weapon-Seeker had somehow found and appropriated. What was it? How had it exploded the head of Stephen the Strong-Armed?

That was to be worked out another time. Meanwhile, he had his chance. It might not last long; he had no idea when the panic might subside and a patrol of warriors be sent back to investigate. He stepped carefully across the red stream flowing from the fallen man's neck. Squatting down in front of the dropped spear, he managed to get a grip on it with his bound hands and rose, holding it awkwardly behind him.

No time to cut his bonds. Not here. "Uncle Thomas," he called. "We can get away. We have a chance now. Come on, get up!"

The wounded band captain stared up at him without comprehension. "—corridors like you've never seen or imagined," he continued in a low monotone. "Glow lamps that aren't on foreheads. Corridors filled with glow lamps. Corridors and corridors and corridors—"

For a moment, Eric considered. The man would be a heavy liability in fast travel. But he couldn't desert him. This was his last surviving relative, the only person who didn't consider him an outlaw and a thing. And, shattered as he was, also still his captain.

"Get up!" he said again. "Thomas the Trap-Smasher, get up! That's an order, a warrior's order. Get up!"

As he'd hoped, his uncle responded to the old command. He managed to get his legs under his body, and strained against them, but it was no use. He didn't have the energy to rise.

CASTING apprehensive looks over his shoulder at the entrance to the storage burrow, Eric ran to the struggling man. Working backwards, he managed to get one end of the spear under the crook of his uncle's arm. Then, using his own hip as a fulcrum, he levered hard at the other end.

It was painful, slippery work, since he couldn't bring all of his muscles into play and it was difficult to see what he was doing. In between efforts, he gasped out orders to "Get up, get up, get *up*, damn you!" At last the end of the spear went all the way down. His uncle was on his feet, staggering, but at least on his feet.

Dragging the spear awkwardly, Eric urged and butted him out of the place. The great central burrow was empty of people. Weapons, pots, and miscellaneous possessions lay strewn about where they had been dropped. The finished structure of the Stage stood deserted in front of the royal mound. And some time before, the bodies of his uncle's wives had evidently been removed.

The chief and the other leaders had bolted to the left once they had clawed their way out of the storage burrow. They had apparently run past the scaffold structure and picked up the rest of Mankind in their panic.

Eric turned right.

His uncle was a problem. Thomas the Trap-Smasher kept coming to a bewildered halt. Again and again he began the story of his long-ago journey to the burrows of the strange, distant tribe. Eric had to push against him to keep him moving.

Once they were in the outlying corridors, he felt better. But not until they had made many turns, passed dozens of branches and were well into completely uninhabited burrows, did he feel he could stop and saw himself free of his bonds on the point of the spear. He did the same for his uncle. Then, throwing the Trap-Smasher's left arm across his own shoulders and clutching him tightly about the waist, he started off again. It was slow going; his uncle was a heavy man, but the more distance they could put between themselves and Mankind, the better.

But distance where? Where should they go? He pondered the problem as they tottered together down the silent, branching corridors. One place was as good as another.

There was nowhere that they would be welcome. Just keep going.

He may have muttered his questions aloud. To his surprise, Thomas the Trap-Smasher suddenly said in an entirely coherent but very weak voice: "The doorway to Monster territory, Eric. Make for the doorway to Monster territory where you went to make your Theft."

"Why?" Eric asked. "What can we do there?"

There was no answer. His uncle's head fell forward on his chest. He was evidently sliding into a stupor again. And yet, somehow, as long as Eric's encircling arm pulled at his body, the man's legs kept moving forward. There was some residual stamina and a warrior's determination in him yet.

Monster territory. Was there more safety for them there now than they could find among human beings?

Very well then, the doorway to Monster territory. They would have to come around in a wide arc through many corridors to get to it, but Eric knew the way. He was Eric the Eye, after all, he told himself; it was his business always to know the way.

But was it? He had not enjoyed the formal initiation into manhood that was the usual aftermath of a successful Theft. Without that, perhaps he was still Eric the Only, still a boy and an initiate. No, he knew what he was. He was Eric the Outlaw, nothing else.

He was an outlaw, without a home and a people. And, except for the dying man he pulled along, everyone's hand was henceforth against him.

CHAPTER NINE

THOMAS the Trap-Smasher had been badly injured in the surprise attack that had wiped out his band. Ordinarily, he would have had his wounds carefully dressed by the cleverness and accumulated experience of Sarah the Sickness-Healer. Under the circumstances, however, Sarah had done the reverse.

Now, the strain of escape and the forced headlong flight that followed it had emptied his body of its last resources. His eyes were glazed and his strong, shoulders hung slack. He was a somnambulist walking jerkily in the direction of death.

When they stopped to rest, Eric—after listening intently for any sounds of pursuit—had washed his uncle's wounds carefully with water from the canteens and had bound the uglier gashes with strips torn from a knapsack. It was all he knew how to do—warrior's first aid. A woman's advanced therapeutic knowledge was needed for anything more complicated.

Not that it would have made very much difference by this time. The Trap-Smasher was too far-gone.

Eric felt desperate at the thought of being left alone forever in the dark, uninhabited corridors. He tried to force water and bits of food upon his uncle. The man's head rolled back, nourishment dribbling carelessly down from both sides of his mouth. He was breathing lightly and very rapidly. His body had grown quite warm by the time they stopped.

Eric himself ate ravenously. It was his first meal in a long, long while. He kept staring at his recumbent uncle and trying to work out a line of action that would do some good. In the end, he had thought of nothing better than to hitch the man's arm up over his shoulder again and to keep going in the direction of Monster territory.

Once erect, the Trap-Smasher's feet began walking again, but with a dragging, soggy quality that became more and more pronounced. After a while, Eric had to come to a halt; he had the feeling that he was hauling dead weight.

When he tried to lower his uncle to the floor of the burrow, he found that the body had become almost completely limp. Thomas lay on his back, his eyes staring without curiosity at the rounded ceiling upon which his forehead glow-lamp outlined a bright circular patch.

The heartbeat was very, very faint.

"Eric," he heard a weak voice say. He raised his eyes from his uncle's chest and looked at the painfully working mouth.

"Yes, uncle?"

"I'm sorry—about—what I got you into. I had—no right. Your life—after all—your life. You—my wives—the band. I led—death—everyone. I'm sorry."

Eric fought hard to holdback his tears. "It was for a reason, Uncle Thomas," he said. "We had a cause. It wasn't just you. The cause failed."

There was a hideous cackle from the prone man. For a moment, Eric thought it was a death rattle. Then he realized that it had been a laugh, but such a laugh as he had never heard before.

"A cause?" the Trap-Smasher gasped. "A cause? Do you know—do you—know what—the cause was? I wanted— wanted to be chief. Chief. The only—only way I could—do it—Alien-science—the Strangers—a cause. Everyone—the killings—I wanted to—to be chief. *Chief!*"

He went rigid as he coughed out the last word. Then slowly, like flesh turning into liquid, he relaxed.

He was dead.

ERIC stared at the body a long time. It didn't make any difference, he found. The numbness in his mind remained. There was a great, paralyzed spot in the center of his brain that was unable to think or to feel.

In the end, he shook himself, bent down and grabbed the body by the shoulders. Walking backwards, he dragged it in the direction of Monster territory.

Something he had to do. The duty of anyone who lived in the burrows when death occurred in his neighborhood. Now it filled time and used up energies that he might otherwise have expended in thoughts, which were agonizing.

The energies, which it demanded were almost more than he was capable of at this point. His uncle had been a heavy, well built man. Eric found that he had to stop at the end of almost every curving corridor and get his breath back

He finally arrived at the doorway, grateful for the fact that his uncle had died so relatively close to it. He also felt he understood why this had been suggested as their destination. Thomas the Trap-Smasher had known he had little time left. His nephew would have the responsibility of sewering him. He had tried to make it as easy for Eric as possible by going the greater part of the distance on his own feet.

There was a fresh-water pipe in the wall near the doorway to Monster territory. And wherever there was a fresh-water pipe, the Monsters were likely to have laid a sewer pipe nearby. It was down this, probably, that the men killed in the battle with Stephen the Strong-Armed's band had been disposed of much earlier. And it was down this that Thomas had known his remains must also go—the closest point at which his nephew could sewer him in comparative safety.

This much, at least, he had done for Eric's benefit.

Eric located the fresh-water pipe without much difficulty. There was a constant low rumbling and gurgling underfoot, and—at the spot where it was most pronounced—he found the slab in the floor cut at the cost of infinite labor by some past generation of Mankind. Near it, after the slab was lifted, was another, much thicker pipe, large enough to carry two men abreast. Like the other one, the hard stuff of the burrow floor had been scraped away so that a joint lay exposed.

Opening the joint was another matter. Eric had seen it done many times by his elders, but this was his own first attempt. It was a tricky business of tugging a heavy covering plate first right, then left, and getting his fingers under the rim and pulling at just the right moment.

THE joint opened at last, and the incredible stink of Monster sewage poured out as the liquid swirled darkly by. Death had always been associated in Eric's mind with this stink, since the pipe carried not only the Monster's waste matter but also that of Mankind, collected from its burrows every week by the old women who were too feeble for any other work. All that was not alive or useful was carried to the nearest Monster sewer pipe, all that might decay and foul the burrows. And that included, of course, the bodies of the dead.

Eric stripped his uncle's body of all useful gear as he had seen the women do many times. Then he dragged it to the hole in the burrow floor and held it by one arm for a moment as the current of the sewage caught it. He repeated as much of the ceremony as he could remember, concluding with the words: *"And therefore, O ancestors, I beg you to receive the body of this member of Mankind, Thomas the Trap-Smasher, a warrior of the first rank, a band captain of renown and the father of nine."*

There was usually another line or so—*"Take him to you and keep him with you until the time when the Monsters have been destroyed utterly and the Earth is ours again. Then shall you and he and all human beings who have ever lived rise from the sewers and joyously walk the surface of our world forever."* But this, after all, was a pure Ancestor-science passage; and his uncle had died fighting Ancestor-science. What was the Alien-science equivalent? And it likely to be any more potent, any less full of falsehood? In the end, Eric omitted those last two lines.

He let go of the stiffening arm.

The body shot away and down the pipe. Thomas the Trap-Smasher was gone, he was gone for all time, the way Eric reasoned now. He was dead and sewered, and that was that.

Eric closed the joint, pulled the slab down and stamped it into place.

He was completely alone. An outlaw who could expect nothing from other human beings but death by slow torture. He had no companions, no home, no beliefs of any sort. His uncle's last words still lay, in all their stern ugliness, at the bottom of his mind. *"I wanted to—to be chief."*

IT was bad enough to discover that the religion on which he had been raised was a mere prop to the power of the chieftainship, that the mysterious Female Society was completely unable to see into a person's future. But to find out that his uncle's thoughtful antagonism to such nonsense was based on nothing more substantial than simple personal ambition, an ambition murderously unscrupulous and willing to sacrifice anybody who trusted him—well, what was there left to believe in, to base a life upon?

Had his father and mother been any less gullible than the most naive child in the burrows? They had sacrificed themselves—for what? For one superstition as opposed to another, for the secret political maneuvers of this person as opposed to that.

Not for him. He would be free. He laughed, bitterly and self-consciously. He had to be free. There was no choice: he was an outlaw.

Eric walked a few steps and put his hands on the door to Monster territory. To shift it out of its socket was a hard job for one man. He strained and tore his fingers; finally he managed it. The door came away and he deposited it carefully on the floor of the burrow.

He stared at it for a while, trying to figure out a way of getting it back after he'd passed through the doorway. No, a single man just couldn't do that from the other side. He'd have to leave the doorway open, an incredible social crime.

Well, he couldn't commit a crime any more. He was beyond all rules made by human communities. Ahead lay the glaring white light that he and his kind feared so much. Into this he would go. Here, where there were no illusions to be found and no help to be expected, here he would make his solitary outlaw home.

Behind him lay the dark, safe, intricate burrows. They were tunnels, Eric knew now, in the walls that surrounded Monster territory. Men lived in these walls, and shivered, and were ignorant, and made fools of each other. He could no longer do these things—he had to face the Monsters. He wanted to face them and destroy them.

It was like one of the roaches in the storage burrow declaring war on a cook who came in to make the evening meal for Mankind. The cook would roar with laughter at such a thought. Who knew what went on in the mind of a roach—and who cared? Yet the roach would enjoy two special advantages. He had once and for all stopped crawling greedily and aimlessly with his own kind, and the enemy he had selected could regard him with nothing more than heavy oblivious contempt. If he could ever for a moment find one usable weapon and one vital area on which that weapon could be used...

He hefted his two special advantages grimly. Then Eric the Only, the Eye, the Outlaw, Eric the Self-Aware Individual Man, stepped through the doorway into Monster territory.

THE END